Longarm _____ _____ g. He
fired with th_____ _____ ger's
shirtfront. The slicker's gray Stetson fluttered to the
cinders as his corpse sprawled back like a stringless
puppet with its shirt on fire.

Levering another round in the chamber, Longarm
stepped off the walk to stand in a pool of lamplight,
expecting his junior deputies to come running at the
sound of gunplay and not wanting either of them to
mistake him for anyone else with a Winchester held
at port arms.

But his back made a swell target, as he realized
too late—when a gunshot rang out behind him . . .

DON'T MISS THESE
ALL-ACTION WESTERN SERIES
FROM THE BERKLEY PUBLISHING GROUP

THE GUNSMITH by J. R. Roberts
> Clint Adams was a legend among lawmen, outlaws, and ladies. They called him . . . the Gunsmith.

LONGARM by Tabor Evans
> The popular long-running series about U.S. Deputy Marshal Long—his life, his loves, his fight for justice.

LONE STAR by Wesley Ellis
> The blazing adventures of Jessica Starbuck and the martial arts master, Ki. Over eight million copies in print.

SLOCUM by Jake Logan
> Today's longest-running action Western. John Slocum rides a deadly trail of hot blood and cold steel.

TABOR EVANS

LONGARM

AND THE HIGH ROLLERS

JOVE BOOKS, NEW YORK

LONGARM AND THE HIGH ROLLERS

A Jove Book / published by arrangement with
the author

PRINTING HISTORY
Jove edition / June 1994

ISBN: 0-515-11391-3

A JOVE BOOK®
Jove Books are published by The Berkley Publishing Group,
200 Madison Avenue, New York, New York 10016.
JOVE and the "J" design are trademarks
belonging to Jove Publications, Inc.

PRINTED IN THE UNITED STATES OF AMERICA

10 9 8 7 6 5 4 3 2 1

LONGARM

AND THE
HIGH ROLLERS

Chapter 1

Slippery Elmer Graves was a creature of habits, good and bad. But it might not have mattered so much to that rider of the owlhoot trail had Deputy U.S. Marshal Custis Long taken a less vigorous part in the recent Chinese Riots besetting the mile-high city of Denver.

Neither the local Chinese nor Longarm, as he was more commonly known to friend and foe, had rioted. The mobs running wild all over the West in the wake of the Great Depression of the 1870's had been inspired by the venom spouted by Dennis Kearney, a labor leader and patriot who, having been born and reared in Ireland, desired nothing less than a Grand American Union free of foreigners.

Slippery Elmer Graves, born an American citizen for all his faults, had taken no part in the Chinese Riots because he'd been stopping trains up around South Pass at the time. Hence he'd barely heard of the lynchings in Denver, and wouldn't have thought they had any possible bearing on his own furtive career when first he left a load of dusty trail duds and distinctive dirty underwear at one of the many Chinese laundries along Denver's Cherry Creek.

Longarm was only guessing about that distinctive underwear. But he'd heard Slippery Elmer had been spotted over by the stockyards by a reliable drunk, and had pulled the killer's yellow sheets from the files.

Naturally, Longarm had not been the only decent lawman coming to the aid of innocent Orientals being chased by angry mobs. No single civilized gent could have saved the bulk of Denver's pigtailed Sons of Han all by himself. But unlike some of his fellow lawmen, Longarm didn't accept the almost pathetic gratitude of some of the Chinese as his simple due from simple souls. Having met more than one laundry hand who read both the *Denver Post* and *Rocky Mountain News*, Longarm talked to them as if they were human beings of at least average intelligence, and often got intelligent answers from them that tended to mystify even his boss, Marshal William Vail of the Denver District Court. So that Friday afternoon in August, when Miss Iris Fang of the Chop Chop Chinese Laundry near 13th and Walnut asked him to explain exactly what he meant by "Mormon underwear," she got a courteous explanation, even though she was sort of moon-faced and likely as old as thirty.

Resisting the impulse to reach for a smoke in the clean steamy front of the small laundry, Longarm told the Oriental lady on the far side of the white pine counter: "This Utah killer reputed to be holed up here in Denver has been disowned by the Latter-day Saints, or Mormons as we call 'em. I know you've heard they hold odd views on some subjects, but there's nothing in their Book of Mormon that even a Danite could use as an excuse to stop the Union Pacific Flier or blow up U.S. Mail cars, or government postal workers, with dynamite."

The plain but well-proportioned laundress nodded intelligently and said, "I've heard about those Danites, or Avenging Angels, they send out to murder enemies of their Church."

Being fair as well as firm about such matters, Longarm had to reply, "The Danites were disbanded by the Salt Lake Temple, some say after, others say before Brother Brigham

Young died of a burst appendix a few summers back. Their leadership tends to have new revelations from on high more often than some, which may be why they got in so many arguments coming West to begin with, and in recent years they made some changes in their ways. Be that as it may, and say what you will about them wild-eyed Danites, Slippery Elmer was simply a wild youth who showed no signs of mending his ways as he got older and tougher. So when his first few dozen victims were fellow Mormons, his own Utah neighbors declared him a wanted outlaw. Now, being he's better known where he grew up than he might be in other parts, he's been raising Ned in parts he's less known in. We figure by this time he must have spent most of the loot of that last train robbery. So we'd sure like to nail him before he robs anyone else. He works alone and mean, and they call him Slippery Elmer because he's left few witnesses alive to point him out and sort of slips between the cracks of politer society between jobs. He doesn't drink in low-down saloons or frequent even high-toned houses of ill repute. So those few times he's been spotted over by the stockyards could mean he's planning something involving a train out of Denver. We figure he likes to sneak aboard the train of his choice disguised as one of the brake crew, replacing one of the real crew along the line and simply braking the train to an unscheduled stop, way out yonder where he's left his own camp with some getaway riding stock."

The Chinese gal suddenly smiled, showing nice teeth, and told him, "My word, I think I picture it, and I've never seen a train robbery in my life. But you were going to explain about that unusual underwear, Deputy Long. Don't Mormons wear the same sort of underwear as the rest of you long-nosed devils?"

Longarm chuckled indulgently and passed on the chance to ask about Chinee unmentionables. "Nope. That's one of them odd Mormon notions I mentioned before. They don't smoke, drink, or indulge in tea or coffee either. Somehow, coming West from where the Prophet Joseph met up with an angel under a York State apple tree, they came up with their own celestial design for underwear, male or female. It's always white, with neatly hemmed square openings over them parts most folks are more apt to keep private even while wearing underwear."

Iris Fang suddenly brightened. "You mean even over the nipples? I mean, where even a man has nipples? I *thought* that seemed a little odd as I was sorting out his wash the other day, but who am I to wonder why any of you strange people act so . . . strange."

Since she'd been bold, or innocent, enough to come right out and mention nipples in mixed company, Longarm felt encouraged to say, "Might we be talking about white long underwear with a square opening down below, suitable for various natural matters to take place without shucking out of it, ma'am?"

She nodded. "I don't think it would be as much fun, but I suppose it would be possible. You say this man robs trains and kills people too?"

"He does, likely wearing the same sort of underwear he grew up in. Folks are funny that way. A mighty mean Indian I know still wears a cross around his neck and sneaks into church to attend Papist masses and sneak some commun-ion bread, just because they sprinkled him as Jerome, or Geronimo in Spanish, many a moon back. Slippery Elmer ain't been to any Mormon services here in Denver. We've been watching. But I come up with that Mormon underwear as a long shot, and you say I guessed right?"

The bright laundress pursed her lips. "If the man I know as Mister Palmer is the same Mormon. I don't have any of his laundry on hand right now. But I can dig out the address of that boardinghouse he had us send his last delivery to. What might this Slippery Elmer look like?"

4

"Ordinary. I'll come back and tell you if we're aimed right after I pay your customer a visit at his address."

So she got out a bundle of slips covered with Chinee lettering, found a pencil, and wrote down the address of a nearby boardinghouse for Longarm in English.

He thanked her, then asked if she might have any other laundry due to be delivered fairly close to what might be Slippery Elmer's chosen hideout.

She smiled incredulously. "I could easily wrap some old papers in our usual wrapper, but do you really think you could pass for a Ching-Ching China Boy, Deputy Long?"

Longarm said, "My friends call me Custis, and who's to say what an honest but unemployed cuss might or might not do for some drinking money? I'll tell you what, Miss Iris. You make me up a fake laundry delivery and let me worry about how convincing I can deliver it, hear?"

So she did, laughing as she fashioned a large but almost weightless bundle of crumpled newspaper, wrapped in thinner but stronger-waxed blue tissue, bound with butcher's twine and bearing one of her distinctive tags.

She begged him to come back and tell her how it had all turned out. When he assured her he would, she insisted she meant to hold him to that promise, even if she wasn't that pretty young thing who ought to be ashamed of herself at the Golden Dragon.

That last odd remark gave Longarm something other than Slippery Elmer to worry about as he legged it the short distance to the address she'd given him.

As he neared the boardinghouse, Longarm could see at a glance the galoot was paying a lot of money to stay in that mustard-yellow and spinach-trimmed carpenter's gothic with mansard roof. It was on a double-sized and tree-shaded lot, surrounded by a freshly painted picket fence.

A yard dog was chained to a stake, fortunately for the both of them, as Longarm opened the front gate and traipsed up

5

the sandstone walk in his tobacco-tweed suit, dark pancaked Stetson, and flat-heeled cavalry boots. He wondered who might be watching him from inside, attracted to any number of lace-curtained windows by the yapping yaller mutt.

He'd deliberately unbuttoned his frock coat, it being August in spite of the altitude, so anyone could see he wasn't packing hardwear on his right hip. The double-action .44-40 riding cross-draw in his left hip was hidden from anyone inside by the bulky package he held over it, blocking his gun hand.

As he mounted the front steps, the front door swung open and a formidable-looking old pouter pigeon wearing purple gingham and hair warned him she had no more rooms to let.

Longarm went on up anyway, removing his hat with his free hand as he said, "I ain't in the market for room and board, ma'am. I got a delivery for your Mister Palmer from the Chop Chop Chinese Laundry."

The dowager scowled. "They have a white man delivering their laundry now? Well, I never, but hand it over and I'll see he gets it, young man."

Longarm put his hat back on as he politely but firmly replied, "They told me no tickee no washee, ma'am. I find this unusual as you do. But Miss Iris, over to Chop Chop, allowed she'd give me half off on some shirts she just ironed for me if I'd run this over and collect the money. So I dasn't deliver without collecting, hear?"

The landlady said, "Wait here. I'll see if he's in and wants to do business on this porch, for land's sake!"

So Longarm had plenty of time to get set and try to look really dumb by the time the old bat sent a suspicious character with some obvious suspicions of his own out to confront him.

The boarder answering to the name that went with Mormon underwear was a reedy little squirt in his late thirties or early forties. He wouldn't have stood near as tall as Longarm even

6

if he'd had on boots instead of a pair of bedroom mules. He was also wearing pajama pants and a maroon velveteen smoking jacket. You couldn't tell whether he had Mormon underwear on under his lounging duds. But his gun was likely under that folded copy of the *Post* rather than riding under the sashed-up smoking jacket.

"What's got into those fool Chinee? I don't have any laundry I ain't already paid for!" he grumbled. Then Longarm simply busted the right forearm under that innocent-looking but oddly draped edition of the *Post* with the muzzle of the .44-40 he'd apparently produced from thin air.

As Slippery Elmer's ass chased his clunking Schofield revolver to the painted planks, Longarm kicked him all the way flat, then kicked the six-gun off into the foundation shrubbery before he hunkered down to say not unkindly, "You were right about the laundry. I was out to take you alive, and as you can plainly see, I have. I'd be U.S. Marshal Custis Long, and you know damned well what you're under arrest for, Slippery Elmer."

His prisoner told him he was mistaken. Meanwhile, the old pouter pigeon in purple came out on the porch with a broom to knock Longarm's hat off and announce she meant to sweep him clean off her property.

Longarm blocked her second swing with his pistol barrel, stinging her palms pretty good, and warned her she'd spend the night in jail along with the federal prisoner he was trying to arrest in one damn piece.

That got her to at least stop swinging. Then he told her and others now gaping out the doorway at him who Slippery Elmer really was.

The injured outlaw kept insisting in an injured tone that he was a victim of false arrest who meant to sue everyone up to and including President Rutherford B. Hayes for all the pain and humiliation the infernal U.S. Government was putting him through.

7

Longarm hauled him to his feet by the one sound wrist he'd handcuffed to his own as he warned, "You'll suffer more if we compound that fracture by needless wrestling, pard. I only hit you hard enough to disarm you for certain without the bones having to come out the skin. So behave your fool self and your right wing will likely heal in time for your hanging. Let's go. It's payday as well as late, and I mean to carry you over to the Federal House of Detention before the streets get really crowded."

The killer protested, "I can't walk that far afoot in just my bedroom slippers! Won't you at least let me dress more proper up in my room?"

Longarm considered. He didn't hold with needless cruelty, since he felt punishment was up to the judge and jury to decide. But on the other hand, they could surely make a mile or less on sandstone and cobbles before even those sissy slippers wore through. So he shook his head and said, "We'll send someone for all your possibles later, if only to search for some loot. Meanwhile, it's late and I promised a lady I'd come back and tell her how we made out with you. She never said how late she stayed open."

Chapter 2

"But how did you know it was him?" asked Iris Fang after Longarm had assured her Slippery Elmer was safely stowed away for as long as it might take to grant him as long a trial, and rope, as he had any right to expect.

By this time they were out back in her kitchen, so she could stir-fry some eggs, pork, and greens in the cool shade of a summer eve with the winds off the front ranges to the west. They'd tied Longarm up with paperwork for a time at the House of Detention. So he'd expected her to be closed by the time he got done, but as he'd promised, he'd mosied over. She'd confided, as she opened up and hauled him in, that her laundry had closed officially and she'd sent her hired help/relatives home, holding off on her own supper in the hope that he'd join her. She had him sipping tea, laced with gin, as she got down to greasing her wok and tossing the raw makings in to sizzle. He'd eaten enough Chinese grub to know you couldn't warm it over without it tasting like gum arabic. So he didn't ask her to explain her late start cooking.

Instead he said, "I saw right off that Palmer fit the general description we had on Slippery Elmer. But the clincher was the way he came out the door aiming the *Denver Post* at me. A gent disturbed as he's reading the paper during working hours might come out with the paper clutched in one hand, or draped over one arm with his exposed hand making sure it stayed put. But I've yet to see anyone carry a newspaper draped neat but loose across his right forearm and what looked like an unusually long index finger. So seeing I had my own six-gun drawn under that fake laundry delivery, I thought it best to disarm him before one of us got hurt. He gave up on pretending he was innocent by the time the doc was setting his busted arm in the prison dispensary. Reckon he felt he had to say who he was so he could admit what he really thought of me. I dasn't repeat what he thought about you helping me track him down, Miss Iris. But if you ever need a favor from Marshal Billy Vail at the Federal Building, you just say so, hear?"

She dryly observed the U.S. Constitution and those few lawmen sworn to uphold it had already done right by her and her kith and kin. Then she asked in a more thoughtful tone, "Do you think we have to worry about *his* tong, ah, Custis?"

Longarm assured her, "He don't have no kith and kin on this side of the Great Divide. I told you before how little the folks Elmer grew up among regard him today. But since I see no call for you to testify at his coming trial, I can make sure you ain't mentioned in any court papers if you like."

She commenced to scoop steaming supper from her big shallow wok into blue willow bowls as she declared, "I'd like that very much. But won't they ask you how you knew where to find him, Custis?"

To which he could only modestly reply, "They're used to me being smart. I'll just say I was put on his trail by hitherto reliable informants, and should anyone ask who that might have been, I can stand on the rights of privileged information. That's what they call such secrets when a lawyer, a priest, or even a lawman refuses to rat on someone who'd been told he could be trusted not to do so."

She put their bowls on the tiny table she'd seated him at, observing, "It seems to me you'd have done us all a favor and added to your reputation if you'd simply shot the rascal when he came out with a gun of his own leveled at you!"

Longarm ignored the old army mess-kit fork she'd politely placed on the table near his teacup, and reached for the chopsticks standing upright in a glass tumbler instead. "Such thoughts did cross my mind at the time. They often do. But I'm paid to bring 'em in, not execute 'em. So that's what I do, when I can."

She arched a thoughtful brow as he dug in with the chopsticks, but politely refrained from commenting on his table manners as she quietly observed, "From what I've read about you in the papers, you bring in less than half of them alive, though."

He tasted a gob of mishmashed egg, pork, and pea-pod, the trick being to go for small nibbles with each grab of the chopstick, as he made a wry face and said, "Reporter Crawford from the *Post* tends to glorify me as Denver's answer to the late Wild Bill. The ones willing to come along quiet don't make the front page as a rule. As for some I've had to bring back on ice now and again, it don't weigh too heavy on my conscience as long as I know they gave me no choice. There are a few lawmen who'd rather gun an outlaw than mess with him. There's some who think it makes 'em heroic to gun a poor cuss they have the drop on. But I've always felt it's enough to bring 'em in as best I can and leave it to the judge whether they live or die. I sure do admire these sort of scrambled eggs, Miss Iris. Is it true some of your folks admire eggs a hundred years old, instead of fresh like these?"

She sighed. "That's an exaggeration, like saying something is a hundred times better than something else. The preserved eggs you speak of are seldom even a full year old. The original idea was to keep eggs from spoiling as they were shipped from one part of my old country to another. In time, some people developed a taste for them, the way your people developed appetites for, let us face it, clotted and decaying mammary secretions."

Longarm wrinkled his nose. "I'd forgot how disgusting you folks find milk, butter, or worse yet, cheese. I'll take your word on ancient eggs tasting better than they sound, and mayhaps it's just as well neither one of us shares the Hebrew opinion of pork. For you sure fry it swell."

She leaned across the table to spike his small teacup with a good shot of gin as she murmured morosely, "There's plenty more. I know better than to offer you any of the ghastly glop my people call dessert."

He sipped some gin with a spot of tea in it along with the wad of pork and greens he'd been saving to protect his tongue. Women of any race seemed to like neat gin better than most men did. He figured it had something to do with the smell. In the hopes of preserving his head in the morning from the afterglow of juniper berries, Longarm said, "I suspect I've had some of that Chinese bean curd with sugar and spice sprinkled over it, Miss Iris. The fruits that taste something like perfume smells are called leeky cheese, ain't they?"

She laughed and told him that was close enough. "It seems you have been trying to find out if it is true what they say about Chinese girls. That is, if you've been close enough to some Daughter of Han to be served preserved litchi all the way from Canton. So tell me, kindly Occidental sage, *is* it true what they say?"

Longarm swallowed thoughtfully lest he say something less than sage. Then he shrugged. "Being a Chinese gal, you'd be in as good a position to answer, if gossiping about such matters was a matter of vital importance."

12

She sipped more of her own gin laced with tea. She somehow managed to look less plain while insisting, "You're surely not going to tell me you don't know! As I told you before, it's all over town about you and that waitress from the Golden Dragon!"

He said, "That sure was swell, ma'am. You say we got some of that bean-curd custard fixed as well?"

She rose, not too steadily, in her apron and ecru silk pajamas as she murmured, "I've yet to see one of your kind finish a serving."

He didn't ask how much she'd been drinking on an empty stomach, as she'd waited for him after closing hours. He wondered if he was feeling drunk himself, or only respectful to a lady, as he stripped away that thin tan silk with his eyes while she bent over the other way, fussing with that Oriental custard.

He'd about concluded she had a great ass when she turned back to face him with her plain moon face sort of wistful above the plates of bean-curd dessert. Her tits didn't seem as plain now that she'd let the button loops of her high-collared blouse fall loose. He knew she wasn't too drunk to know how informally she was acting. The question before the house was would a man be a total polecat taking advantage of a gal that drunk as well as old, or would he be an insulting brute if he left a lady feeling frustrated and foolish after she'd almost come right out and asked for it.

He thought about that both ways as he somehow managed to get down a dessert she'd implied he'd find bland and slimy. If a polite Chinese had been offered, say, apple pie with cheddar cheese, he might manage about as well. But in either case, it seemed to depend a lot on what you'd gotten used to growing up. Mexican food could be just as odd when they hit you with something less logical than chili con carne or hot tamales. He found himself asking his Oriental hostess if she'd ever tried alligator pears in vinegar or chicken baked in bittersweet chocolate Monterrey-style.

She said she didn't like any sort of chocolate, and just couldn't picture a pear shaped like an alligator. She stared across at him owlishly. "In my country pears are round, not the funny shape they have here on the Golden Mountain. Why do you people say we have our vaginas set criss-cross instead of the way they are, Custis?"

He managed not to blush—it wasn't easy—as he calmly replied, "It's doubtless because we don't see one another naked as often, Miss Iris." Then he sighed and added, "I wish you wouldn't do that, ma'am," as the shapely but far from pretty, or sober, laundress got up from the table to gravely start disrobing.

There wasn't near as much to take off when one started out in a true Chinese outfit. As she neatly folded and set aside first her linen apron, and then both the top and bottom of her simple silk pajamas, he saw she'd been wearing no underwear of any description and her white socks only rose a few inches above her ankles. She turned a full front view to him, little brown fists on ample hips. He saw that, like some Indian gals, she'd either shaved or plucked the hairs around her love slit—which, in this case, ran the same swell way as any others he'd ever seen. So he got to his own feet and moved over to join her, warning her even as he took her in his tweed-covered arms that she had about three full seconds to decided whether she meant it or not.

She swore at him in Cantonese and threw her plump bare arms up and around him to crank his face down to her own for a big wet kiss. He kissed back, as most men would have, but might have said something more Victorian when they came up for air if she hadn't sobbed, "What is the matter with you! Don't you think I'm as pretty as that little snip from the Golden Dragon?"

As a matter of fact he didn't, and he still didn't after he'd swept her up and followed her directions back to a sandalwood-perfumed bedchamber draped in red muslin, where she proceeded to show him she knew one hell of a lot more about screwing.

That pretty little thing from the Golden Dragon had acted all flustered as a man sat on a bed beside her shucking his own duds. But as Iris Fang helped Longarm out of his own underdrawers and caught sight of all he had to offer, she said, "Yum, yum, I'm so glad it's true what they say about American boys!"

He could tell right off she was experienced. She told him later, as they shared a three-for-nickel cheroot, how she'd run off from an arranged marriage with an old but skillful Chinese to seek her fortune in the New World with a younger railroad coolie *she'd* gotten to teach before he'd died on her while still young. Longarm was too polite to ask whether she'd screwed the poor cuss to death. From the way she went down on his poor dong before he could finish his smoke, let alone get his own second wind, he could only thank his lucky stars he was in good shape and hadn't had any for close to a week, thanks to that field job a hard-driving boss had had him on.

Since things were turning out the way they were turning out, he just let her suck him all the way hard again, and paid for her hospitality by pronging her in various positions she swore were new to her, seeing he had it up but couldn't seem to come again no matter how he pounded.

She took it as a compliment, as plain gals with great figures tended to take it when a man seemed anxious to come in them more than once. But for his part he'd gotten past the pleasure into showing off and wondering, even as he was thrusting in and out of her, what in the world all the fuss was about.

Some kindly sage had once observed, likely in French, that the only times a man was completely sane were right after a good meal and a satisfactory screw. So Longarm was feeling sane as hell when the poor old gal he was screwing started to cry.

He stopped, took it out, and snuggled her naked flesh closer to his as he asked, even though he knew, what was eating her.

She said, "Oh, Custis, I know you're going to think I'm some sort of spiteful tease, but there was more to you than met the eye and, well, would you be terribly cross with me if we called it a night? I have to get up so early in the morning, and you've worn me out so much with your big strong body that I . . . Oh, whatever must you think of me, since it was my idea to start all this?"

He kissed the part in her luxurious black hair and told her he was mighty glad she'd started it. "I needed it as much as you could have. But since you brought it up, it might be wise to quit whilst we're ahead. Lord only knows what your neighbors might say if they spied me leaving after midnight!"

She kissed him in a more sisterly way, and said she was so happy he was an understanding gentleman as well as a long-nosed devil with the biggest organ-grinder she'd ever had in her at either end.

She made him more gin-spiked tea as he got dressed again. He was feeling a tad stiff in joints he hadn't noticed they'd both been bending so peculiarly. Then they parted friendly, well inside her dark front entrance, and he was on his way with the night still fairly young.

But he never headed for the Black Cat or the Parthenon Saloon in downtown Denver. A wise man grabbed for such brass rings as the merry-go-round might allow. So still walking a tad stiff, but not hailing a hansom cab lest he show up the same way, Longarm walked the better part of a mile up to Sherman Street, to present himself, a tad weary but moving more naturally, in the doorway of an imposing brownstone mansion.

The brown-haired young widow woman who answered his discreet tapping wearing her nightcap and dressing gown

16

looked surprised as well as relieved to see him standing there. He had a sheepish smile on his face and a bunch of straw flowers from a street vendor in his hand. She gasped, "Oh, Custis, I'd given up on you and gone to bed with a good book. Or a long book, at any rate. You know why I've been laying there upstairs reading the same damned page over and over, don't you?"

He stepped inside and kissed her in an almost brotherly way before he said, "I told you this morning I had to track down that train robber, honey."

She took the straw flowers with one eyebrow cocked at him as she replied, "I know what you *said* you might be doing, well into this night, if not *all* night, after I told you I'd be indisposed with the curse of the moon for the next few nights."

As he followed her along the darkened hallway he protested in an injured tone, "You'll be reading about it in the morning papers if you don't believe me. I caught Slippery Elmer earlier this evening. You know how much paper-pushing I'm saddled with after I make even a less important arrest. Look here, woman, did you really think I was out looking for another gal just because your sweet little ring-dang-doo was out of commission?"

She called him a sweet and understanding thing, and led him on up to her bedroom suite, where she set the flowers in a vase and put him on her four-poster to tell her the whole tale while she made hot chocolate on her spirit burner.

He left out the parts that might have unsettled her, and by the time he had Slippery Elmer and all that paperwork taken care of, they'd finished the chocolate and she was yawning fit to bust.

She confessed she'd been staying awake with tense nerves and lots of floor-pacing, picturing him in the arms of that sassy blond barmaid at the Parthenon. After he'd assured her, truthfully, he'd been nowhere near the sass, the somewhat older but prettier young widow woman yawned again and declared, "I'm about to fall asleep sitting up. Do you think you could behave yourself in the same bed with me if I . . . took care of you with just a little tune on the French horn, dear?"

He yawned himself, and soberly replied, "That hardly seems fair to you, honey. Why don't we just turn in platonically for a change? I doubt it'll hurt us as long as we don't overdo it."

So they did, with more flannel covering her shapely charms than usual as she snuggled her head on his bare shoulder, repeating all that guff about him being such a sensitive soul under all that rawhide and whipcord exterior.

It was easy to act sensitive around women when you weren't sure you'd ever get the poor thing up again.

Chapter 3

Longarm enjoyed ham and eggs in bed, declining another chance at a unilateral orgasm because it was dumb to shoot one's wad at breakfast when you didn't know whom you might be meeting for lunch.

Marshall Vail made everyone work until noon on Saturday, and got all hot and bothered when a deputy showed up after nine. So Longarm was crossing the lawns of the big old State Capitol while the mockingbirds were still cussing the sunrise. He legged it down Colfax to the lower level the business district of Denver sat on, and spied a pair of stenographer gals reporting for work just ahead of him when he scaled the granite side steps of the Denver Federal Building.

The inside steps were marble, and led him up to the marshal's office he worked out of, as often and as far away as possible. But with a recently arrested outlaw to be arraigned, and with that widow woman keeping a more anxious eye than usual on him, he figured he was looking forward to at least a few mighty dull days.

He figured wrong. Young Henry, the squirt who played the typewriter out front, told Longarm to go right on back to the marshal's private office. So he did, to find the older, shorter, and far fatter Marshal Billy Vail had already filled his sunlit but dark-paneled chamber with a blue haze of pungent cigar smoke. Since Longarm only paid a nickel for three of the long thin cheroots he favored, he'd never in this world been able to figure out what those shorter fat creations Billy smoked could be made of. He'd always suspected sunflower stems cured in chickenshit. So he'd lit a smoke of his own in self-defense on his way back to Vail's office. It only helped a little as he blew the smoke out his own nose and exhaled.

Billy Vail seldom invited anyone to sit down. But there was one big leather chair set up on Longarm's side of the cluttered desk. So he just sat down and leaned back, waiting for his boss to tell him he had court duty coming up.

Vail never did. He muttered, "Mind your damned ashes on my damned rug. The onionskin I'm looking for is somewhere in this damned pile. The docs tell me you busted both bones in that train robber's skinny arm and now he's all swole up and feeling poorly."

"Or pretending to," Longarm pointed out. "I told him last night he'd likely not appear before Judge Dickerson this side of Monday noon or even Tuesday, the docket being sort of crowded this summer. As for busting that arm, I could have just shot him point-blank, since our gun muzzles were close to overlapping at the time and we both knew he was wanted on hanging charges."

Vail said, "Nobody here is complaining you abused any innocent children, old son. You done good, and that was smart of you to trace a cuss living so respectably by way of his dirty underwear. I only mentioned his likely having to spend some time in the hospital because you may as well be doing something useful as we wait for Slippery Elmer's first day in court."

Longarm brightened. "Who might you want me to bring in from where, and could we manage me, say, a full week away from Denver with all its cares and woes?"

Vail cocked a bushy brow. "Didn't know that brown-haired society gal down from near my place was sore at you again."

Longarm didn't answer. He was pretty good at getting folks to say more than they might want to about their private lives himself.

Vail chuckled. "Never mind. I just sent Smiley and Dutch up to Holy Cross to pick up One-Eyed Jack McBride. They came back empty-handed. Worse yet, the barkeep who'd tipped us off about the killer being in town had been killed before Smiley and Dutch got to talk to him. How do you like it so far?"

Longarm flicked tobacco ash on the rug in case there might be carpet mites as he observed thoughtfully, "I've heard of One-Eyed Jack. He's supposed to be a mighty ugly customer. I've heard of the *mountain* called Holy Cross. It's supposed to be mighty pretty, just the other side of the Divide from Leadville. Never heard tell of any *town* called Holy Cross, though."

Vail nodded his bullet head and explained, "That's because there was no such town till mighty recent. That silver lode Leadville's famous for seems to run clean under the Continental Divide, and some prospectors struck an outcrop there. Rumor has it the lode's higher grade than anyone's found on this side of the Divide, and we all know how rich Silver Dollar Tabor and Leadville Brown wound up mining as little as forty ounces of silver to the ton."

Vail picked up a wanted flier and blew smoke at it as if to dust it off. "They hit higher grade yellow-green chloride of silver, contaminated with copper instead of lead, to the northwest. They named their mine and then their mining town after the mountain you just mentioned. It's off a ways from the town, but you know how close distant peaks can look in the high country on a clear day. Be that as it may, we both know how many fortune hunters, hunting various ways, crowd into any uncertain source of wealth. The barkeep interested in the bounty on One-Eyed Jack told us the rascal was wheeling and dealing with the other high rollers up that way. So I sent Smiley and Dutch, like I said. They're good old boys on your average case. But One-Eyed Jack ain't average. To begin with, we don't even know what the son of a bitch *looks* like!"

Longarm nodded soberly. "I've gone over his yellow sheets. He's more famous as a drifting gambler than a killer, and he might never have made it to our lists of federal wants if he hadn't gunned that Indian agent and made off with them Indian Agency funds the poor simp had put in the pot after he'd been dealt a royal flush."

Vail nodded grimly. "That's the way One-Eyed Jack's been known to make a literal killing more than once. We figure he's more often content to just cheat the others in the game out of any funds they have on 'em. It's when he figures he has a really ripe plum to pick that he's been known to get so nasty. He has to get nasty because a sucker ain't likely to bet a company payroll or agency funds unless he knows for certain he's been dealt a winning hand."

Longarm nodded. "It's an unusually dirty way to win at cards if you ask me. So I'll be proud to go arrest the son of a bitch if you'd like to tell me how to get there and how to identify him. There was nothing on the sheets I saw that told me even whether he was old, young, fat, or thin, or even how many eyes he might have. I can come up with many a way for a gambling man to be named for the jack of hearts or the jack of spades, neither of which show more than one eye to anyone."

Vail said, "Don't teach your granny how to suck eggs. I naturally told Smiley and Dutch to watch out for a man with only one eye or for a two-eyed gambling man pointed out by our informant. But the new silver strike is crawling with high-rolling gamblers as well as tinhorns from all over, and like I said, our informative barkeep was in no condition to point anybody out. Nobody up that way seems to know who might have shot him late one night as he stepped out back to take a leak. Smiley and Dutch were able to eliminate a couple of dozen locals who couldn't have been lurking out back at the time. I got their damn list here somewheres."

Longarm shrugged. "Do you want me to work on who might have gunned down a barkeep or search for One-Eyed Jack? There's no law of nature saying an unrecognized but wanted man couldn't have been sitting innocent as a big-ass bird whilst a personal enemy of that barkeep, or a confederate he'd hired, blew the poor bastard away in the dark."

Vail beamed across the desk at him. "That's why I send you out on the tougher ones, old son. I admire a lawman who can think as sneaky as most crooks. You're still going to want a list of likely and less likely suspects, and I'd best give you a typed-up rundown on that murdered informant too. Why don't you go see about arranging your short but complicated travels whilst I have Henry type up all the shit you might need. You'll find the new mining camp on this year's Bureau of Mines survey. Beats the shit out of me how you might get there from, say, the end of the rails at Leadville, though."

Longarm rose to his considerable height as he allowed he'd best begin by figuring out where he was going. The Bureau of Mines had a branch office just down the corridor. Longarm wasn't even thinking about the short and frequent rail connections to Leadville, not a hundred miles to the southwest on Denver's side of the Divide.

Since it was Saturday morning and rank had its privileges, he found a female version of Henry holding the fort for the Bureau of Mines down the corridor. But while she was as young and pale as their own clerk-typist, Longarm had to allow she looked a whole lot prettier as she sat there in her summer-weight blue bodice with pencils stuck in her piled-up hair and regarded him warily through her glasses. When she still seemed reluctant, even though he'd explained it all twice, Longarm growled, "What do you want from me, a search warrant? Ain't this a federal office open to all interested parties, and ain't I a federal agent interested in looking at only one infernal mining claim plat?"

She gulped and said, "I know who you are and all about you, ah, Custis Long. I don't know what you might have heard about *me,* but I assure you I have nothing in common with a certain well-endowed blonde from the stenographers' pool!"

Longarm smiled sheepishly down at her. "I can imagine what you might have heard about Miss Bubbles and me, ma'am. But you have my word I ain't never done nothing to any lady working around her that she never said I could. As to my having ulterior motives in wanting you to take me back to your file room, I only need a gander at a contour map of the high country betwixt Leadville and Holy Cross."

When he saw she didn't seem convinced, he smiled thinly and dryly asked, "Do you really think you're as good-looking as all that?"

She blinked behind her specs. "I beg your pardon?"

"I make better than five hundred a year, with eight or ten years towards my pension as long as I don't get my fool self fired. I'll allow you ain't so bad-looking, if you'll allow a man would have to be out of his head with raging desire to risk a decent job for a grab at anything you could ever produce against your own free will!"

She was blushing like a rose as she stammered, "I never said I was afraid you'd *attack* me, good sir!"

So he said, "*Bueno.* I ain't worried about you attacking me neither. Could I please see them infernal claim plats now, ma'am?"

She got up from behind her typewriter to show him back to a small file room with one frosted window. Neither one of them got fresh with each other as she found the wide flat drawer they were looking for and hauled it out for him. The area Longarm was interested in lay no more than two sheets of sepia-and-black-printed paper down.

Place names, boundaries, and such were in black ink over the paler brown contour lines Longarm had hoped to find. There sure were lots of them between Leadville Township and the more freely inked new mining camp called Holy Cross. So Longarm got out his notebook to make note of the landmarks and natural ways over the Continental Divide. Mining claims, a lot of mining claims, were peppered over a chart of this scale as bitty numbers. He knew each number went with a larger-scale chart showing more limited areas if a body wanted to dig through those files. But he didn't. Billy Vail wanted him to hunt for One-Eyed Jack, not a silver mine.

As he put his notes away he thanked the gal and shut the big drawer for her with his own hip. As they went back out front she blurted out almost wistfully, "Why, you're not as fresh as they told me you might be after all! I confess this leaves me feeling sort of foolish. Now that I see you've behaved like a perfect gentleman after I as much as accused you of . . . you know."

To which Longarm could only reply, with a gallant tick of his hat brim, "I was raised to act like a perfect gent around a perfect lady, ma'am."

So they parted far friendlier than they'd just met, even though it had been close to fourteen hours since he'd had any. That frisky old gal at the Chop Chop Chinese Laundry had sure left him feeling calm and collected up to now. But the day was still young, and maybe it wouldn't be a bad move to drop in on old Iris Fang again before he had to face all that lonely riding over the Continental Divide.

Chapter 4

He got off the train in Leadville just before sundown, dressed for cross-country riding in faded summer denims and packing his old army McClellan saddle on his free hip. For all his mistakes at Antietam, General G. B. McClellan had designed one mighty handy saddle for a rider with a lot of possibles to carry along with him in the field. Where your average stock saddle had no more than a half-dozen latigo points, the McClellan had all those brass fittings to fasten one's saddlebags, bedroll, Winchester '73, and so on, resulting in a good load, even for a man as big as Longarm.

Fortunately, he knew his way around Leadville, and it wasn't too far to a livery he'd dealt with before on Harrison Avenue. As they stored his McClellan in their tack room for him, they agreed it was too late to head on over the Divide with any stock they might have to hire out. The old-timer he knew there added they'd be able to fix him up better come the Sabbath. For total assholes who hardly ever rode a pony seemed to need one to tear about on when it was Saturday night in Leadville.

Longarm didn't need to ask why. Leadville boasted of eighty-odd saloons, twenty-one gambling houses, thirty-eight

26

restaurants, and no man had ever counted how many whorehouses.

There were nineteen hotels, forty-one boardinghouses that didn't allow whoring, along with three undertakers and the usual smelters, lumber yards, blacksmiths, and such it took to keep a good-sized mining town humming. Longarm had supper across from the opera house, noting they were promising, or threatening, to present *The Flower Girls of Paris* in the near future. He polished off his cherry pie à la mode with plenty of black coffee, and lit up out front to see what might happen next.

What happened next was mighty odd, although not by Leadville standards. You could hear the bagpipes and kettle drums coming long before you could make out the source of all that noise. But then, down the avenue came all sixty-odd members of Tabor's Highland Guards in red tartan kilts with feathered bonnets at a cocky angle as their white goat-hair sporrans swished back and forth down the fronts of their kilts. Tabor was a Scottish name, according to the rich gent, but "General" Tabor didn't seem to be leading his private army that evening. Some said he'd taken to spending a lot of his spare time with a pretty grass widow instead of his old time-tested wife, Miss Augusta. Since it was hardly a federal matter, Longarm neither knew nor cared whether it was true old Silver Dollar had been behind the arrest of Elizabeth Doe's dull husband in a house of ill repute. The Denver P.D. had never raided the place before, and it sure had given an outraged as well as shapely young wife plenty of justification for an uncontested divorce. Only Silver Dollar Tabor himself knew how he planned to get shed of the formidable Augusta. Nobody figured on her letting him go without a fight.

Once the Tabor Highland Guards had bagpiped by, Longarm crossed over to the opera house, saw the sign in the ticket window offered standing room only, and headed on away.

The street lighting could be tricky as the big fat Colorado stars winked on in the purple skies of an early evening in high country. It got trickier as one wandered farther from the center of town. So Longarm barely noticed the small white blur out in the center of the avenue as a coach and four swept grandly around a corner at full gallop while some woman screamed louder than your average banshee.

Then Longarm was moving, faster than most expected a man his size could move, and his low heels still made the difference as he swept up the little kid in the center of the roadway and barely made it on across, with two wheel hubs nearly wiping his ass in turn as they never slowed down.

The little gal baby he'd snatched from the jaws of death in the form of pounding hooves was bawling fit to bust as he made it as far as the walk across the way. He knew it would be a waste of time to tell her he wasn't fixing to eat her. So he just looked about for another responsible adult to take her off his hands.

Nobody with more sense than himself could cross the avenue till half a dozen other reckless riders got done with it. Longarm neither knew nor cared whether they were chasing that coach and four or just losing a race with it. Heavy-wheeled vehicles had the edge tearing down a grade that way.

Then, as the dust still hung in the cool night air, the screaming mother of the screaming baby girl he was holding caught up with them to take her off his hands, sobbing, "Oh, my God, how can I ever thank you, sir? I don't know how she got out of our quarters but—"

"Why don't you get her back inside then?" Longarm said, unable to resist adding, "Would anyone here like to bet me this tyke ain't within six months of her second birthday?"

There were no takers among the gathering crowd. The young mother sighed and said, "She's eighteen months old as of last week. I see you have children of your own, good sir?"

Longarm found himself blurting out, "Not that I know of!" with more heat than the question called for. The calico-clad young brunette with the little baby in her arms was only pretty in a sort of slender rawboned way, and so he repeated his suggestion she get the both of them somewhere warmer before they both caught some ague.

She thanked him some more anyway, then ran back across the wide avenue with her wayward daughter. Longarm heard someone refer to her as Widow Wallace while explaining the rescue to someone else.

As several onlookers commenced to tell Longarm how brave he'd been, the tall deputy growled, "Never mind all that. Nobody would've had to act so foolish if that coach and four hadn't been driven by some total asshole just now!"

A townsman volunteered, "Oh, that would have been Sky Kirby, the famous sportsman. He always sweeps through town sort of grand. Takes a heap of noise to attract any attention here in Leadville!"

Longarm said, "I've noticed. I've heard of that windy tinhorn as well. He must be afraid the bigger boys won't let him in the game if he forgets to act childish."

Another townsman laughed. "Ain't nobody bigger than Sky Kirby when it comes to playing most anything for high stakes. They say he won't sit down to a table where the stakes don't commence at ten dollars a chip. So I'd hardly call him a tinhorn."

Longarm growled, "You call him what *you* want and I'll call him what *I* want. It's been nice talking to you all. But I never came to town to admire Leadville's answer to Bet-A-Million Gates or Diamond Jim. I still have to find me a place to sleep for the night before I scout up my own sort of foolishness."

As he strode off aimlessly, he saw that that skinny gal with the dangerously active child had lit up the second-story quarters she and her kid had climbed to by way of an outside flight of pine steps. He wondered idly why he'd been paying that much attention.

He wasn't paying much attention to the early evening crowd out on the avenue with him till he spotted that coach and four parked out front of a fancy hotel, with the reins being held by a grown man instead of a hitching post. As he crossed over, he saw the cuss was dressed in a military greatcoat and kepi that would have made a Mexican general feel a tad underdressed. So Longarm figured he had to be the doorman who went with the grand hotel.

As he joined the doorman by the lathered leaders of the matched quartet of cordovan trotters, Longarm said, "Evening. I've a bone to pick with the driver of this coach and four. Might he be a guest at this establishment?"

The doorman pursed his lips as if he'd never seen sun-faded denim before and replied, "No. Mister Kirby asked me to hold his horses so he could present himself to a lady from Pueblo we *do* have as a guest tonight. You can't go in there dressed like that. But if you wait out here they should be coming out any minute, and you'll be able to make your complaint to Mister Kirby here on the walk."

Longarm snorted in amused disgust and started to push on by. The doorman warned, "Be careful, cowboy. You're wading in over your head, and if our house dick doesn't put you back in your place, Mister Sky Kirby's personal bodyguards play even rougher!"

Longarm glanced about, nodded, and said, "I was wondering about that cavalry squad tear-assing after this coach and four a few minutes ago. But who might be holding their horses and where . . . Right, across the way, pretending to be just spitting and whittling on the covered walk with one holding all their ponies down by the corner. Were they dressed too shabby for your fancy lobby too?"

The doorman shrugged and muttered not unkindly, "Do yourself a favor and don't mess with Sky Kirby, cowboy. I don't know what you think he owes you. But take it from me, you don't want to approach him with that surly attitude."

Longarm said he wasn't acting half as disgusted as he really felt, and headed for the entrance as behind him that doorman blew a tin whistle in a series of dots and dashes. So Longarm wasn't surprised when a shorter but mighty solid-looking cuss in a checked suit met him just inside the marble-pillared lobby. "Only guests and their properly dressed visitors are allowed to use our front entrance, cowboy," he snapped. "If you've something to deliver, take it around to the back."

Longarm smiled thinly and said, "Get out of my way. I don't mean to say that again."

Before the house dick could respond, Longarm saw the somewhat older and softer-looking cuss who'd been driving that coach and four was headed their way with an even softer and somewhat younger redhead on one elbow. As Longarm started to say something a mite more polite, the house dick between them reached under his checked coat. So Longarm whipped out his .44-40 and clubbed the man to the marble floor before things could get really silly.

The couple with the unconscious house dick at their feet froze in place as if they'd been asked to pose for a tintype. Sky Kirby's poker face only paled a shade as he quietly said, "I'm not armed. If it's only money you're after . . ."

"This ain't a robbery. I'm a concerned citizen," Longarm said, lowering his six-gun politely to his side. "If you had a lick of common sense and the eyes God gave a bat, you'd have been driving slower through the center of town. You surely saw me snatch that kid right out from under your leader's hooves!"

The dapper older man looked relieved and replied, "Oh, was that you? I was in a hurry for reasons any gentleman ought to be able to grasp. I would have stopped had I run over that brat. But I didn't, thanks to you. So why don't you fuss at the parents who'd allow a toddler to cross the avenue alone

31

after dark? What do you want from me, a signed confession I was anxious to pick up Miss Clara here?"

"Clara Drakmanton," the redhead murmured with a gracious nod at Longarm before she turned back to her escort. "If the boy saved our evening by preventing some sort of trouble, I feel we ought to reward him, don't you?"

Sky Kirby nodded, but it was he alone who fished out a twenty-dollar gold piece and flipped it at Longarm as if he were tossing a peanut to a monkey.

Longarm caught the flashing coin left-handed without thinking. Before he could throw it back, with a remark about Sky Kirby's pissant arrogance, he had a smarter notion, and contented himself with just muttering, too low for a lady to make out the words, as the two of them swept grandly around both him and the house dick at his feet.

The poor cuss Longarm had flattened seemed to be waking up sore as hell about something. So Longarm felt it was time to quit while he was ahead.

He ducked out a side exit he knew from having been in there before, that time in his own frock coat with a younger lady on his own elbow. A man had to think ahead when he knew half a dozen others might be out front with orders to do most anything.

Chapter 5

Twenty dollars was either a gesture of contempt from a high roller or two weeks' salary for a top hand, depending on how you studied it. Longarm had time to study on his own recent manners as well while he legged it back the way he'd just come. He was glad everyone back there had taken him for a cowhand in his practical riding duds. He knew he'd likely be out of town before anyone found out who he was. He knew Billy Vail shared his distaste for blowhard bullyboys. But old Billy would never approve of a senior deputy of his pistol-whipping anyone he wasn't fixing to charge with some greater offense than being offensive.

When he got to the outside stairs above the shuttered dress shop, Longarm got out the gold coin, and made sure he was smiling politely as he knocked on the door at the head of the stairs. A long time later that same slender brunette came to the door with her long hair down and her willowy body wrapped in a polka-dot blue dressing gown. She smelled as if she'd just had a quick cold bath as well. She was even prettier with her face fresh scrubbed and calmed down.

She said, "Oh, it's you! I don't know what to say. I mean I know I said I'd do anything for you, but we're very poor and . . ."

"This might help," Longarm said, handing her the coin instead of flipping it. "It comes with a message from that gent who almost ran down your kid. Fair is fair, and I had to agree you never should have let her stray out in the streets like that."

She sighed. "I'd just come home from work. I was serving a cup of coffee to the girl I pay to look after Sarah when I'm at the shop and, well, I don't know when or how she got out while we were having coffee and cake. I didn't notice she was gone until we were both at the foot of the stairs out there and I saw her tiny form out in the middle of the avenue!"

Longarm nodded. "They'll do things like that at that age. They're just big enough to run wild and still too little to understand our well-meant words of warning. Tell a two-year-old a choo choo train is coming and you can bet he'll run for the tracks. But all's well as ends well. So it's been nice talking to you, and I'd better get it on down the road."

But she insisted he let her coffee and cake him at least. So he followed her on into her small, sparsely furnished, but neatly kept four rooms set up shotgun-style along one side of the upstairs hall.

When he asked, she said the baby was asleep in her own small room, or securely encaged in a crib at any rate. So she set him on a big leather sofa in her modest parlor while she fetched marble cake and still-warm coffee from her small kitchen.

As they sat side by side, eating and sipping off her low-slung coffee table of pulpwood stained to look like mahogany, she told him more about herself than he'd ever asked. Her name was Pansy Wallace née Culhane. Her mining man had fallen down the shaft of the Little Pittsburgh, owned by a couple of Dutch gents but grubstaked by the Tabors.

"Augusta Tabor is a living saint!" declared Pansy Wallace, as if she felt she was an authority on such matters. Longarm had to agree the plain-faced but imposing Gussie Tabor had behaved more Christian than some when he heard she'd taken in the widow and orphan of a miner she'd hardly known, made Silver Dollar pay for a grand funeral with bagpipes, and then grubstaked Pansy to her own dressmaking business a couple of streets away.

Longarm was too polite to stare about rudely. But as if she could read his mind, the young widow explained, "Every penny I make goes back into expanding my trade. I've sent all the way to Saint Louis for my dress patterns, and all our seams are lock-stitched with real silk all the way from New Jersey! I mean to fashion the best made-to-measure wear in the Rocky Mountains and make sure my Sarah never has to marry a mining man when she grows up!"

Longarm sipped some coffee and observed, "Libby Custer would no doubt agree with you on cavalry men as well, Miss Pansy. None of us menfolk deserve a pretty young wife if we don't aim to stick around till she's an old lady."

The young widow sighed. "There are times when I do feel awfully cross with Peter for falling down that shaft like that. Of course he never meant to, and I'm sure he felt mighty vexed just before he hit bottom. But there are times, especially at night when my feet feel so cold, I almost feel he did it to spite me. You see, we'd had a silly spat the night before he was killed and, well, I made him sleep on this very sofa, albeit we and all our furnishings were upslope at the time. Do you think it's true what they say about Hod Tabor and that awful Baby Doe?"

Longarm couldn't see what Silver Dollar Tabor's tawny-haired play-pretty could possibly have to do with another gal's man falling down a mine shaft after a night on the sofa. But he knew women had to be able to make such connections, for they so often seemed to make them in the middle of a conversation. Idle conversation with a gal was a lot like riding a cutting horse through a stampede. A man had to be set for sudden shifts in direction.

So he shrugged and said, "I can see why some call Elizabeth Doe Baby, having met her socially a time or two. She's way more petite as well as way younger than Miss Augusta Tabor, albeit if I had to make such a grim choice, I'd likely go with the older but far wiser one. She may be plain, but she ain't deformed, and you ain't the first to tell me she's a decent old gal. I can't see Baby Doe lifting one finger for another gal in trouble, if she had the brains to notice. Beautiful women don't need to develop their brains. So not all of 'em do. Libby Custer's sort of stupid in her own sweet way, now that I think back on beautiful women I've met up with."

Pansy Wallace sighed. "Baby Doe must be really something to look at then. You'd be surprised on how tough it can be to get by on looks alone, unless you have no pride to go with them. Augusta Tabor was the only one who offered to help us unselfishly, with no strings attached, and if that Baby Doe ever shows her face in my dress shop, I'll just snatch her bald-headed!"

Longarm sighed. "She'd likely just stand there and let you, wondering what on earth you were doing that for. Like I said, the poor thing's about as bright as a sheep and, well, it's usually the sheep herder they put in jail for her sort of behavior."

Pansy laughed so hard she spilt coffee on her dressing gown, and had to wipe her knees with a napkin as she told him he was awful and confessed she found the picture amusing as well as dirty. Then she said, "It's just not fair. They say the Tabors started out as humble storekeepers, with Augusta doing most of the work whilst Hod swapped tall stories with the boys. It was Miss Augusta, not her free and easy husband, who made hungry prospectors sign written contracts giving Hod shares in any claims they found a trace of color in. It was Augusta, not Hod, who nailed Hook and Rische down on paper just before they hit pay dirt, and it was her idea to buy shares in Meyer and Harrison's big silver smelter."

Longarm repeated what he'd said about Miss Augusta looking smart.

Pansy insisted, "She's nice too! But now, thanks to her brains and elbow grease, all those early years when nobody like Baby Doe would have looked at old Hod Tabor, he's gotten rich enough to be Lieutenant Governor and steal other men's wives with no more effort or conscience than a schoolboy swiping apples!"

"I heard William Doe's arrest was a political favor, ma'am," he replied, politely covering a yawn before he observed, "That's the way this old world has always been run, and to be fair, it's a heap tougher to pin a vice rap on a man who stays home nights. Old Silver Dollar Tabor may be quicker than most to take advantage of a rival's weaknesses, but at least he stays within the very limits of the law."

He drained the last of his cup and added, "Mayhaps it's just as well the law allows that much slack. There wouldn't be prisons to hold all the rascals who lie, cheat, and steal without pulling a gun on anyone. We got enough of the just plain dumb and ornery ones to keep locked away as it is."

When she started to refill his cup he quickly said, "No, thanks, ma'am. It ain't that I don't enjoy your company. But you'll be stuck with more of mine than you bargained for if I fall asleep on this sofa before I can find me a place to spend the night. You see, I was looking for a room to hire when I met you and little Sarah out front. But it's getting late and so . . ."

"You're welcome to stay here for the night!" she blurted out, looking away as she quickly added, "Out here on this sofa, as you suggested, I mean. I mean, it's not as if we're strangers now, and I'm sure we can both be trusted."

He couldn't resist asking, "Trusted to do what, ma'am?"

She blushed and stared down at the dark leather between them as she murmured, "To behave ourselves, of course. I don't mind telling you there've been times I wished I wasn't

37

so well behaved. My man left me alone on this earth a young woman, after they'd told us I could never have any more children after Sarah's birth, which was sort of a complicated procedure. But I wasn't raised the way that Baby Doe seems to have been raised, so . . ."

"Are you trying to say you'd like to take me to bed with you, Miss Pansy?" he asked, grabbing her wrist as she tried to slap him. "If you're only telling me all about your horny and barren condition to tease me, I'd say that was a mighty mean way to treat any guest. So now the question before the house is do I go or stay. Like I said, it's getting late and this has gotten downright uncomfortable, for me at least!"

She sighed, and he felt the arm he was holding go limp as she softly told him, "For me as well. It's been so long and you smell so manly in those clean sunwashed denims, but can I *trust* you, sir?"

He said, "My pals call me Custis, and if you mean you don't want me bragging around town, I got to get on over the mountains to the west slope come morning. If you meant could you trust me to take it out ahead of time, all bets are off."

She laughed sort of crazy and said she'd known right off he'd had a lot of experience on parlor sofas. But when he reeled her in for a kiss and ran his free hand inside her dressing gown she protested, "Not on this sofa! If I'm going to do this at all I want to do it right, in my bed, without anything in our way!"

So that was how they did it. As they undressed side by side in the dark as if they'd been married up a spell, he knew he wasn't going to have to spend the night out on that sofa after all. He knew she'd been having similar thoughts when, a few moments later, as he was entering her stark naked body with his own for the first time, she suddenly clutched at him, digging in her nails, and threw her long willowy legs around his bare waist to bite down hard with her vaginal muscles, sobbing up at him in the dark, "Oh, yes! Deep as it will go and damn you, Peter, for all these lonely nights you've put me through, with this pussy just aching for . . . My God, I'm coming!"

He moved in her faster, skillfully, even as she pleaded for him to stop and let her get herself back. So he had her moaning like an alley cat in heat and out of her mind with pure passion by the time he came himself, enjoying it so much he had to gasp, "Powder River and let her buck! For if she'd have had wings I'd have screwed her flying!"

The slender, slithery gal he had nailed to the mattress with his still-stiff organ-grinder laughed despite herself, and asked if he always said such romantic things to a lady he was fucking.

Seeing he had her enough at ease to speak frankly now, he told her, "Only when I really like 'em. I save the mush for the schoolmarms who bust into tears afterwards and threaten to slash their own wrists after acting so depraved. That's what some gals call it when you make 'em enjoy it, depraved."

She laughed. "I've never felt more depraved in my life, and I can't begin to thank you enough. About that silly business when I forgot who you really were and called you by another man's name, darling . . ."

He kissed her gently. "We've all done it. I mind the time I was snowed in with a good-natured but sort of plain gal and there was this copy of the *Police Gazette* with a picture of Miss Ellen Terry on the cover, and . . . Never mind. I don't usually discuss other folks in bed with a pal. But you started it, and my point is that it's natural to imagine someone you really want while coming with what's available."

She hugged him tighter with her thighs and pressed her small firm breast up against his bare chest as she soberly asked who he'd been pretending he was coming in before.

He began to move again, in time with the contractions of her warm wet innards, as he told her, "Nobody but you, Miss

39

Pansy. You ain't a plain gal I'm just screwing as a sort of port in the storm. I am screwing you personal and enjoying every square inch of your sweet bare hide. I'd enjoy it more if we could light your bed lamp and I could see what I was doing to you as I slid it in and out!"

She gasped, "Oh, I couldn't, Custis. I'm not as experienced as you seem to be, and even when my husband was alive we never did it naked with the lights on!"

He didn't insist. So it was Pansy who asked, while they were at it dog-style in the dark, if he'd ever done it this way when he could see the poor girl in such a ridiculous position.

He thrust harder, saying, "Yep. It's inspiring as all get out to part your cheeks like this, and I'd likely come even faster if I was watching your pretty little asshole winking up at me as I pounded you to glory!"

She gasped in dismay, begged him not to talk so dirty, then said he might as well strike a match if he wanted to see her that badly.

So he lit the lamp, and after she'd come again with her eyes shut tight as she could get them, Pansy suddenly stared up, then down between their naked bellies, and sobbed, "Oh, my God, I can see your naked penis as you bob your hips between my thighs, and it wasn't like this with Peter at all! Dear God, I'm screwing a strange man and enjoying every thrust of his strange cock! I never meant to betray my poor husband by enjoying another man *this* much!"

He moved her into another position she moaned she'd never been screwed in before, as he said soothingly, "You ain't betraying nobody. Old Silver Dollar Tabor is betraying the wife who stood by him many a year by doing things like this with his sassy grass widow. But you ain't married or even divorced from your true love, Miss Pansy. You just have to get by without him as best you can, and there ain't no sin in coming good if you mean to come at all!"

So she said she wanted to get on top and he let her. She laughed like a mean little kid and bounced like one on a pony, with the saddlehorn set well back, while she confided, "I'm glad you got me to talk dirty and do it with the lamp lit, Custis. For it does feel grand to just let yourself go and do it for pleasure and . . . Do you know what? I still feel the same way about poor Peter. How can I love and miss one man while I've got another one's cock up inside me and enjoying every inch of it?"

He rolled her over on her back so he could hook an elbow under her knees on either side as they both enjoyed the end a lot. Then he rolled off, fumbled a smoke from his shirt on a nearby chair, and snuggled her to his side while he lit it. Then he told her, "It's swell when all our warm feelings go together, honey. But you can love somebody without screwing 'em and vice versa. Nobody would expect a body to starve to death just because the one they used to dine with can't come to supper no more. I don't know whether widows who carry their mourning far as bragging, the way Queen Victoria and Libby Custer do, get a little slap and tickle on the sly. But if they don't, it just ain't healthy to act so unnatural."

She snuggled closer and sighed, "I know. I'm ashamed to tell even you some of the ways I've tried to relieve myself down there. You're the first man I've given myself to since Peter was killed, and I know I should be feeling more dramatic. I mean, I expected to fall madly in love or feel beside myself with shame if ever I got up the nerve to bed you. I mean the you I half expected to come along, albeit not this soon and . . . Oh, Custis, I don't know what I mean!"

He took a drag on his cheroot, ran his free palm down her flank, and said, "That's all right. I know what you mean. There was this gal up Montana way, we called her Roping Sally because she was the only woman I ever met who could rope better than me."

"Were you in love with her, Custis?" the woman he'd just made love to quietly asked.

He said, "It was too soon to tell. Seems we'd just got to be pals when she was murdered cruelly by crooks out to steal some nearby Indian lands. I got the ones as murdered her, and we buried her in a pretty place where harebells and pasqueflowers bloom in their seasons. My point is that as we lowered her down, I just couldn't believe I'd never kiss her sweet lips or enjoy the jiggles of her grand hard-riding hips again. I couldn't imagine myself in bed with anyone else just then. But of course I was, with another gal who looked, talked, and jiggled nothing like my lost Roping Sally."

"And so you just forgot the dead cowgirl and got on with it?" asked the mining man's young widow.

Longarm shook his head and began to toy with her tailbone as he replied, "Nope. I recall her fondly as ever, and I can almost feel her bigger and even firmer ass even as we speak. But her ass ain't here. It never will be, and your ass is just as swell, in another way entire. So what do you suggest we do about it?"

She said, "You might start with putting out that cheroot. Then I mean to suck your cock. It's not his cock, but it's an awfully sweet cock, and if you're really leaving in the morning I don't aim to miss a single opportunity tonight!"

Meanwhile, out on the dark State Street, a couple of city blocks away, a shadowy figure was reporting to another shadow seated in a coach and four. The bodyguard said, "We've scouted high and we've scouted low, Boss. But there just ain't nobody answering to your description booked into any hotel or boardinghouse in town. What if he's holed up in some private home?"

Sky Kirby grumbled, "Get out there and scout some more. Wherever that saddle tramp is, he made me look bad in front of a woman and I want him dead as a turd in a milk bucket!"

Chapter 6

The slopes all around Leadville had been logged for pit props and firewood, riddled with try-holes, overgrazed by milk goats, and powdered with smelter soot. But heavy industry tended to be concentrated as well as ugly in an age powered by steam and sweat. So the mountains commenced to pretty up again by the time Longarm had been on the trail a couple of hours, riding a jug-headed buckskin and leading a more lightly packed roan.

They'd told him back there at the livery that both brutes had been over the trail to the west slope and back more than once. As the narrowing trail wound up through fluttering second-growth aspen at an ever steeper angle, he began to buy that. Riding stock used to packing a load across more gentle grades tended to pant and balk, all wall-eyed, when a rider asked them to scramble up slopes where the loose gravel flew a long silent way before clattering against anything down yonder.

But while the hairpin turns over hogback ridges were a bother, and there were stretches where you had to sort of guess your way across patches of slickrock, the day had dawned glorious with hardly a cloud in the oversized blue sky, and the higher peaks to the west smiled down in the bright sunlight in a way that justified the old Indian name of Shining Mountains. There wasn't near as much snow this late into summer, of course. But there was always some in the more shaded clefts of the higher slopes. That was how the one to the north called Holy Cross had gotten its name. A lot of times the steep alpine horn was white with snow all over. But when the summer sun licked down to the dark bedrock, you could see an almost perfect big white cross of deeper snow, rooted in monstrous and almost artificial-looking clefts carved by Mother Nature for her own good reasons.

Nobody had noticed until recently, after the Utes who'd clung so long to the western slopes had screwed up at White River and given the army a fine excuse to run them clean out of the Central Rockies. But now schoolkids were being told the pine-cone-prying mountain cross-beaks had bent their poor beaks out of shape trying to pull the nails out of that big white cross on one face of Holy Cross Mountain. Folks were always saying things like that to kids.

Thinking about kids got a man to thinking back to little Sarah crying in the next room while her momma was trying to come once more in the morning. Thinking about that naturally got him to thinking about how he'd promised good old Pansy he'd neither forget how good it had felt to screw her, nor refrain from screwing for the rest of his natural life once he rode on.

But then he wryly remembered, as he lit a cheroot and rode on, how some old pals stuck in your memory better than others, so that a man lying alone in a sleeping bag and trying to add up his total score would suddenly recall an old pal he'd forgotten completely and have to backtrack and count over, all confounded.

Sometimes the ones you'd forgotten had been damned fine lays, once they popped back into your fool head, while others you never forgot might have been troublesome, or teases who'd refused you completely. It was a caution how

44

human memories worked. He could see why he'd never forget Roping Sally, Kim Stover up to the Bitter Creek Range, or those two great-looking gals down Texas way—sweet Jessie and the cruel-hearted hell of a lay called Cyn. But why did he remember that old sex-mad widow woman in that train compartment, or the Chicago gal who flirted with him to distraction and then just lay there like a side of beef, inspiring him to wonder why in thunder she'd ever invited him to bed with her in the first damned place?

He decided it was the unusual gals that stuck in a man's mind, be they unusually good or bad. He'd have never said it to Pansy or any other gal who'd ever been happily married up, but he suspected many a man who'd married up with someone pretty as Miss Ellen Terry lost track of how many perfect nights he got to spend on top of her. He figured that likely accounted for the ability of many a downright ugly whore to make a handsome living off her married johns.

Then he suspected he was going to wind up with a hard-on on top of an already uncomfortable saddle, the McClellan being designed to be easier on the mount's spine than the rider's balls, and got out the onionskins old Henry had given him on the real reason he was up here for. He'd read them all on the train from Denver more than once, but what the hell, he hadn't thought to pack along a copy of Leadville's *Herald Democrat*, and the new *Police Gazette* in his right-hand saddlebag had hardly been edited to cure hard-ons, what with all that gossip about actress gals, the Prince of Wales, and Miss Victoria Woodhull's demands for the vote and open cohabitation. So he perused the blurred carbon copies again, in hopes of noticing a detail he'd missed the last time.

He hadn't. Old Henry wrote tersely as well as grammatically. So there was nothing all that complicated about the story. A poor cuss tending bar in a mushroomed mining town had recognized a customer as the seriously wanted One-Eyed Jack McBride. He'd sent a simple wire to Billy Vail via that

Western Union office back in Leadville. But by the time Smiley and Dutch had arrived to have the informant point the killer out, he'd been killed and . . .

"How did a barkeep in Holy Cross send a telegraph from Leadville, better than a hard day's ride away?" he asked the world about him as he rode ever higher, the aspen having given way to big gloomy spruce that crowded the narrow trail.

There was nothing in the report saying whether the murdered man who'd recognized One-Eyed Jack had sent his telegram personally or had had somebody else send it for him.

Longarm reined in thoughtfully, but didn't try to turn his two ponies on the tricky mountain trail as he gave the matter a tad more thought. "They might or might not remember at the Western Union. But it was better than a week ago at a busy telegraph office, and they're way more likely to recall in Holy Cross whether the dead man took a couple of days off around the time in question."

He rode on, considering how much more likely it was that the dead man had asked some rider headed for Leadville to send the wire for him, and how much more likely it was that that same rider had been the one to betray the reward-seeker to the killer being sought!

"A saddle tramp's share in that bounty on One-Eyed Jack couldn't have been more than a prosperous outlaw might pay to keep his own neck out of the noose. But what happens next?"

He was working on another smoke by the time he decided it might be well worth his time to look into other recent but unsolved deaths where he was heading. Billy Vail had warned him that Holy Cross had yet to incorporate as a township, and that neither Smiley nor Dutch had thought much of the informal town law, a recently retired buff-skinner with a rep for being a brave as well as nasty drunk. But to be fair, even a professional lawman could be forgiven for failing to connect two apparently disconnected killings in a boom town crowded with hardcase strangers. But Longarm knew that had he been One-Eyed Jack, and had some cuss warned him he'd been recognized, neither local gent who knew who he was would have had to fret about getting old and gray!

They burst out of the spruce into a sunny mountain meadow stirrup-deep in emerald orchard grass and blue columbines, as Longarm mused on about it being easier to spot one stranger known to two dead men than to find another informant who could point the killer out a second time. Longarm hunted cross-country a lot like Billy Vail hunted on paper. When you couldn't read all the fine print, you tried to spot the few things that showed up on more than one sheet. Even a glorified town drunk they'd appointed town marshal was likely to have fairly complete files on anything as serious as sudden death.

"Unless they've hired as serious a drinker as old James Butler Hickok," he warned himself aloud. For while old Jim had started out tolerably well, all that bull about him being Wild Bill and all those buckskin outfits he'd learned to wear on the stage back East had made him mighty useless as a lawman toward the end. But the town law ahead, a cuss called Blackfoot Blake according to Smiley and Dutch, had never done anying as wondrous as poor old Hickok to begin with.

But professional courtesy decreed that a lawman riding into another lawman's jurisdiction was supposed to pay him a courtesy call and let him know what was up, whether the other lawman was all that professional or not. But like the old song said, sometimes it was best to just wait till you knew more about it farther along.

Only a few furlongs up the steep trail he passed a wind-twisted juniper, as such cedars were called by Colorado folks, and knew he was nearing the timberline, another not quite accurate part of Rocky Mountain lore. The so-called timberline looked neater from a good ways off. But riding through it, you saw the trees spread out and got more twisted and runty long before you were really out on wide-open alpine shortgrass, cushion plants, lichens, and such. So there were still a few gnomish junipers strewn across a hogback when he topped it to spy bare windswept slopes and worse up ahead.

What was worse than steep bare slopes in high summer was a trail with someone slower ahead as it hairpinned back and forth. Longarm figured that had to be at least two hundred head of calico cows moving close to single file up the god-damned pass ahead in a mile-wide lazy zigzag. The dozen-odd riders herding them, far more than you'd need on more sensible range, were naturally off the trail a few paces higher or lower. So Longarm's first natural thoughts involved just forgetting the blocked trail and forging on up and over that saddle in the sky to the west. But the steep pony trail didn't zig and zag for the hell of it. It followed the natural contours of the slope for miles at a ten-or twelve-percent grade, just about steep enough if you meant to ride any distance. And distances being deceptive in the thin clear air up this way, that saddle was more like another half mile up and five or six west. So Longarm reined in to switch mounts, seeing he had more than the time, and told his brutes as he changed saddles, "They said we'd do well to make her by sundown in any case. Might work as well if we camped below the timberline on the far slope and rode in bright and early instead of more mysteriously at sundown, when rascals such as One-Eyed Jack are more apt to be looking for action."

The roan never argued as he mounted up, gave the lead rope a firm but friendly jerk, and headed on up the trail at an unhurried walk.

A pony walked faster than a cow. So it wasn't long before Longarm was inhaling fresh cow-shit fumes and apparently making the drag rider on the trail ahead of him sort of anxious.

Longarm just kept walking his roan on up as the drag rider reined in, drew his side arm, and fired it straight up. Longarm felt no call to fire back. They were still a good rifle shot apart, and you seldom had to worry about cows stampeding up or down a forty-degree slope. He just kept going until, sure enough, a more important rider than the kid they had riding drag came back along the high side, riding a pinto version of what had to be either the fabled side-hill shorter or a pony well broken in to these mountains. As the apparent straw boss got past their drag rider and dropped down to the trail between Longarm and the herd, Longarm saw it was a woman, and a shapely one, riding astride in batwing chaps that hid her gender better than her black sateen shirt. He saw she let her sun-streaked brown hair fall free from under her telescoped tan Stetson Carlsbad. He knew why. Roping Sally and Jessie Starbuck had both told him hats sat uncertainly on a perch of properly pinned-up hair.

As they got within hailing distance the somewhat weather-beaten but not bad-looking gal called out, "I'd be Edwina Chaffee, a poor relation of the banking Chaffees, and I'm out to get richer by herding this beef to a boom town over on the west slope, seeing the Indians are gone and a lot of hungry miners are making better than a dollar a day. If you're thinking of going into the beef business on your own at my expense, I got a dozen hands and twice that many guns I can call on to discourage you. If you'd like to ride *for* instead of *agin* me, I can pay you a dollar a day and chow if you don't mind changing that saddle."

Longarm started to say who he was and why he was sitting an army saddle despite his well-broken-in range duds. Then he had a slicker notion and declared, "You can't be that poor if you're offering top-hand wages, Miss Edwina. Be that as it may, I've been called a lot of names, but you can call me Virginia."

She looked amused and said, "Virginia is a gal's name. Might you be one of them sissy boys I've heard whispers about?"

To which Longarm could only reply with an easy chuckle, "West-by-God-Virginia gets a mite tedious to say, and The Virginia Kid ain't fit since I blowed out thirty candles a few summers back. I've rid for Captain Goodnight in my time, and more recent for the Diamond K just south of Denver. I hired this saddle along with these ponies just to get over the pass to Holy Cross. If that's the way you and your cows are headed, I'll be proud to keep you company that far. I can't ask you to pay me for being neighborly on the trail, but I may get to acting pouty if I ain't invited for supper this evening."

Edwina laughed, hearty as a man, and said, "Hell, you'll have a cold dinner with warm coffee if we make it up to the pass by noon. Aim to graze 'em some on the fatter grass of yonder saddle, then get 'em down the far slope at least below the timberline before it chills off up here after sundown."

She spun her sure-footed paint around on the tricky trail as she added, "I'll probe no deeper into where you worked, seeing the salary you're demanding."

Longarm trotted after her. As they caught up with that kid riding drag, Edwina called out, "Jeff, this here's . . . Ginger. He'll be with us as far as Holy Cross. You ride on ahead and tell the others. You were bitching about riding drag in in any case."

As the kid nodded at Longarm and rode on grinning, his boss asked, "I hope you don't mind riding drag back here, seeing it ain't dusty as usual and you're set up clumsy for flank riding with that extra pony, no throw rope, and no saddlehorn to hitch it to?"

Longarm shrugged. "I would have been stuck back here in any case, and at least I'm getting free grub and coffee out of it."

Chapter 7

It took a spell, and towards the end Longarm earned his invitation as the grade got ever more gentle near the top and cows, being cows, got to spilling off the trail. Longarm knew they were too far out along the trail for the buckskin he'd been leading to bolt back towards its food and fodder in Leadville. So he turned it loose to follow the ponies close by, as he figured it would want to, so he could cut off more contrary cows as they drifted mostly downhill off the widening pathway. Nobody cared about the ones headed *uphill* in the same general direction as their more sensible herdmates.

Edwina and her dozen whooping and cussing regulars circled and bunched the herd as the trail sort of melted into the flatter saddle between higher and steeper grass to the north and a steeper patch of dusty unmelted snow to the south. Once the cows had settled some, it was easy enough for four riders at a time to keep them grazing the same eight or ten acres by singing to them as they slowly circled. That let the rest of them dismount and study on their own empty innards.

The ambitious Edwina had naturally not hauled a chuck wagon along a hairpin trail that narrowed to less than a yard across in places. Instead she'd brought the trail grub and other supplies on a trio of pack mules. She'd been smart enough to pack some cooking spirits, headed as she was above timberline and into what would likely be the clear-cut slopes of new but thriving mining country. So the hand assigned to dole out their dinner soon had the coffeepot boiling over a blaze of alcohol-soaked lichen and grits. Longarm knew how long it would take to make coffee at this altitude, where water boiled at a lower temperature than even down Denver way, so he took the time to unsaddle and rub down both his livery nags, and then watered them from the vulcanized bags he'd hauled on up from Leadville before he turned them loose, hobbled, to graze with the other stock.

By then the warmed-over coffee was ready, and as she'd promised, old Edwina served the rest out cold, with pork and beans from the can, and with some tolerable sourdough bread to wipe the tin plates clean and wash down with the strong if somewhat tepid coffee.

The four young hands who finished first went to relieve the pals riding drift-guard so they could eat. Longarm knew without asking that Edwina didn't mean to laze up here too long. But he knew from his own cow-herding days how much easier it might be to handle stock that had recently eaten on a strange downhill trail. So he let his own ponies sun themselves bare-backed, as he sat on a granite outcrop and lit a lazy afternoon smoke.

They'd have still moved on sooner had not one of the drift-guards off to the east swung his pony closer to call out, "Another bunch on the shady slope and coming fast, Miss Edwina!"

So Longarm got up too, and followed as Edwina and most of the others mosied east afoot to view the sudden change in the scenery over that way.

The kid had been right about them coming fast. The dotted line of eight riders down below was pushing harder up the zigzagging trail than anyone could herd a cow, or ride a horse without spurring hell out of it. Edwina Chaffee said,

"I'd guess at a cavalry squad in hot pursuit of Ute raiders if any of 'em were in army blue and if that third one back wasn't riding sidesaddle in Kelly green. Outlaws on the run?"

Longarm gripped his cheroot with bared teeth so he could shake his head. "More likely got a late start out of Leadville and aim to make Holy Cross by nightfall."

He didn't argue when Edwina said, "They'll be lucky if they don't founder their mounts getting this high, pushing horseflesh so hard in such thin air."

Longarm found another rock to sit on. She hadn't been lying when it came to the air up this way. He figured he could still run around in circles if he had to. But he didn't have to and meanwhile, just to stand there took more effort than it seemed worth.

Edwina and her riders hunkered down as well. But naturally everybody got back up about half an hour later as the oddly hurried strangers shoved their panting ponies up the last few yards of steeper grade.

As they spotted the spread-out cow folks between them and the more distant cows, they reined in cautiously. Then Sky Kirby, for he was on the second bay back, called out in a hearty tone, "We'd be the Kirby party on our way to Holy Cross, if that's all right with you folks!"

Edwina called back just as friendly, "We'd be the Chaffee bunch, herding such beef as you see to that same mining town. We got no objections to you all riding on to the wide Pacific, if that's your pleasure. But your mounts are fixing to founder if you don't give 'em a decent trail break. We've et all the beans for now, but we still have some coffee if none of you are too proud."

More than one of Kirby's less dapper followers nodded in agreement, but nobody said anything until the jovial gambling man declared he'd follow the little lady's advice about a break and take her up on her generous offer.

Then he spotted Longarm for the first time, and almost lost that salesman's smile as they locked eyes.

Longarm stared back uncaring. He didn't have a federal warrant on the self-inflated snappy dresser, but thought it might be fun to knock him on his ass. It was a bigger disappointment to see the pretty Clara Drakmanton way the hell up in these mountains with such a miserable shit. The afternoon sun made her auburn hair seem spun from newly drawn copper, and she surely filled that green velvet out from where it was tailored around her hips above the loose folds of her sidesaddle skirts. But a man with a lick of self-respect would have gone sloppy seconds to that fat old Prince of Wales instead, and that pretty Princess Alexandra was more likely to have red hair all over.

As the oily Sky Kirby helped his red-haired traveling companion down, Longarm noticed one of Kirby's male followers sidle over to them and bust a gut not looking Longarm's way as he whispered something. Longarm was better than most at reading the way others moved or didn't move within pistol range. But he decided he was only feeling proddy because he just plain didn't like Sky Kirby. The high-rolling gambler could have meant it more ways than one as he shook his head and pointed at some of the spread-out Chaffee hands. Longarm decided he could just as easily be pointing out where he wanted their own mounts hobbled to sun and graze. They just weren't set up to run off Edwina Chaffee's cows, and there was nothing else up this way worth a fight at two-to-one odds.

Longarm didn't feel like listening to any of Sky Kirby's brags. So he sat down a ways off on that same outcrop to light a whole new cheroot while Edwina and her boys made the newcomers welcome around the now-dead coffee fire. He was only mildly surprised when the gal in the much fancier riding duds came over as if to join him, tin cup in hand. A lot of good-looking women were like that when they spotted a man who didn't seem about to jerk off over them.

Longarm had to rise and tick his hat brim, since being deliberately rude could convince some gals you were an asshole in love with them. He then agreed when she said it sure did seem odd to be warmed by an August sun this close to a good forty acres of left-over snow. He didn't get into a lecture on shaded north-facing slopes, or how fresh dew froze on top of such snow fields in the wee small hours, August or not. He just let her sit down, sat down beside her, and waited for her to tell him what she really wanted.

After she'd sipped tepid coffee long enough to see Longarm wasn't likely to propose, she quietly said, "To answer your question, ah . . . Ginger?"

He said, "Ginger's what they been calling me, and I ain't asked you any questions, Miss Clara."

She said, "I'm still going to answer it. I'm not Sky Kirby's play-pretty. I don't belong to any man. I'm a businesswoman with a fair head for business, and there's something off about this trail to the new silver strike at Holy Cross."

He had to ask what she found odd, adding, "Seems as direct a way over the Divide from the headwaters of the Arkansas as I've seen on any survey map, ma'am."

She nodded primly. "So you and Sky Kirby seem to agree. It made sense to me too, on the *map*. But tell me something. Don't you have to dig tons of rock for every ounce of silver, and isn't silver selling for about a dollar an ounce right now?"

Longarm nodded. "They're still arguing about the gold-to-silver ratio in Washington and many a statehouse, ma'am. But I'd say a silver dollar's likely to weigh about an ounce for some time to come. That's how come so many folks pack silver certificates printed on paper of late. Even a week's wages loads one side of your jeans considerable."

She nodded brightly. "That's the point I keep bringing up, and Sky just tells me it's a mere detail I shouldn't worry my pretty little head with. You see, he wants me to look at a chloride claim he won the other night at cards . . ."

"Don't," Longarm said before he'd really thought about how much he ought to advise a total stranger. Then, having said as much as he had, he felt obliged to explain. "They say it takes a gold mine to operate a silver mine, Miss Clara. Unless you already know enough about mining to get by without any man's advice, you're more apt to wind up poor than rich in a mighty tricky game. If we were back in Leadville right now, I might be able to show you a raggedy gent with a sprinkler cart who's paid to wet down and sweep up the streets of the old Cloud City. His name is Abe Lee. They say he made the first silver strike up California Gulch. He hit pay dirt a couple of other times around Leadville. But naturally the bigger boys bought him out every time. They say Silver Dollar Tabor bought out Chicken Bill Lovell for forty grand. Jim Dexter had to sell his Robert E. Lee for thirty, and the new owners produced five hundred thousand worth of ore within three months. But you see, they had the hundred-odd a day it takes to keep your average silver mine operating, or even dry."

She frowned and declared, "I hadn't even considered operating costs! I've been wondering for the last ten miles along that trail how anyone was supposed to haul ore over these mountains and come out ahead!"

Longarm smiled thinly. "You can't. That's another good reason to own a gold mine before you dig for silver. The smelters, railroads, and such come *after* new pay dirt's been proven. It was a tad before my time out here, but they say the first Colorado ore had to be refined all the way back in Saint Lou. The mine owners lost a heap on the deal, of course. The smaller ones were bought out by the bigger ones who could afford to operate in the red until civilization caught up with 'em."

He swept his cheroot expansively across the panoramic drop-off to their east. "If the new strikes around Holy Cross produce enough high grade to matter, you'll see a narrow-gauge laid over this pass, like the one that runs to Durango a ways to our southwest. If it don't, you won't. I can show you ghost towns all over the West that died in their cradles. Nothing to show for all the sweat and heartbreak but a stamping mill, a few gutted storefronts, and a whole lot of holes in the ground. They generally sink try-holes all over a slope before they give up entirely and move on."

"I wonder why Sky Kirby's being so good to me," she murmured half to herself.

Longarm suggested, "As a high roller more famous for high risks at craps and cards, he may feel silver mining is too rich for his blood. You never said exactly what business you were in, ma'am."

She nodded. "That's right, I never did. Do you know that old-timer they call Uncle Billy Stevens back in Leadville, Ginger?"

Longarm replied, "Know who he is. He was the former forty-niner who figured the heavy black sand clogging his gold sluices up in the headwaters of the Arkansas might be silver ore. He took some to an assay man called Wood. Wood got the mysterious black sand to bead as a rich mixture of lead and silver. That's how come they named the place Leadville instead of Silverville, I reckon."

She said, "Uncle Billy told me not to bother hunting pay dirt on the west slope. He said he could sell me all the bothersome silver claims I'd ever want to bother with an hour's ride from the Tabor Opera House."

Longarm chuckled dryly. "Heard Uncle Billy and his partner, Lazy Leiter from Chicago Town, were spending way more time in court than fighting groundwater and sulfur fumes underground. It's a caution how many prospectors can suddenly recall prior claims on a mining property that's showing any profit. Lawyers, mine-supply merchants, and such outright parasites as Sky Kirby and Soapy Smith have always made as much as much or more off mining as ninety-nine out of a hundred mine owners."

He caught himself before he mentioned Leadville's Poker Alice or the notorious Madame Vestal, who some said was the former Confederate spy Belle Siddons. For Clara Drakmanton had as much as told him her interests in these parts were none of his beeswax, and why should an honest innkeeper or purveyor of ladies' notions act so shy?

He had to ask why she was riding all the way to Holy Cross with Sky Kirby if she'd already made up her mind she didn't want to buy his unproven claim. She answered, "We've made a bet. The stakes are in the strongbox at the Claredon House back in Leadville. He's bet me a thousand dollars, at two-to-one odds, I'll want that silver claim enough to buy him out the minute I lay eyes on it."

Longarm declared flatly, "That's a sucker bet if I ever heard one. I've heard Bet-A-Million Gates once wagered on which of two crow birds sitting on a telegraph wire would fly off first. But the wager you just described is just plain loco, Miss Clara! What's to prevent you simply declining his offer, no matter how good it looks, and collecting your winnings back in Leadville? I mean, even if he was to show you a silver-plated grotto, with silver dollars lying all over the floor . . ."

"That's why I put up five hundred paper dollars," she said demurely. "I'd rather walk out of the Claredon House with the fifteen hundred dollars' worth of silver certificates than drag close to a hundred pounds of silver dollars over this long twisty trail!"

Longarm, being better at adding in his head, knew the load would be a tad over ninety pounds, but he felt no call to show off, and knew her point was well taken. He said, "I'd have made that same bet at even money, Miss Clara. So the two of us have to be missing something. I know they say Sky Kirby offers generous odds. But I've yet to hear him called

58

a charitable institution, and you don't look like a lady who could be induced to change her mind against her will, no offense."

Before he could come up with a delicate way to ask how safe she felt about being forced to change her mind *against* her will, the high roller they'd been talking about came over to join them, staring cold as a snake above the smile pasted across his face. Kirby told the gal they would be moving on again directly. As they both rose, Clara said they'd just been talking about getting over this pass easier by rail when or if the Holy Cross claims proved worth it.

Sky Kirby cocked a brow at Longarm and purred, "One of the other Chaffee hands just told me they call you Ginger and assured me you ride herd pretty good. Do you consider yourself an expert on silver claims as well?"

Longarm smiled back just as warmly. "I don't consider myself an expert on cows. But I'm always willing to learn about most anything. You say you got a try-hole on the market, Mister Kirby?"

The high roller snapped, "It's not a try-hole. It's a producing mine following a lode of high-grade chrysolite dead level, with no groundwater to worry about. The bidding starts at a hundred thousand if you're interested in horning in. I'd advise you not to horn in if you're not well heeled and ready to risk it in a game I play for keeps!"

Longarm's eyes never wavered from Kirby's threatening glare as he softly suggested, "Why don't you all mount up and just ride on if you don't want to play with me for keeps?"

Sky Kirby sucked in his breath with a sidewinder hiss as Clara Drakmanton blanched and pleaded, "Stop it, both of you! You're both grown men, not schoolboys walking along a picket fence in front of me and the other little girls, for heaven's sake!"

Longarm had to laugh sheepishly. Kirby just nodded and muttered, "Later, in Holy Cross, with no girls allowed?"

To which Longarm could only reply with as wolfish a smile of his own, "That's where me and them cows are headed, in our own good time. It'll be up to you whether we meet up again down yonder. Like I told you the other night, I don't much care whether I run across . . . gents like you or not."

But as Kirby took Clara Drakmanton's elbow to steer her on to their mounts Longarm remarked, "One thing, though, Kirby. Do we have an understanding betwixt just you and me, or can anyone else play too?"

Kirby laughed almost boyishly, and called back, "I pay my boys well. It's up to them whether they want you to put them out of a job or not. But didn't I just advise you not to horn in, cowboy?"

Chapter 8

The wide and uncertainly mapped complex of ranges called the Rocky Mountains rose greener than the Great Basin to their west or even the High Plains to their east because they ripped open the bellies of high, stingy clouds that hadn't meant to rain anywhere. It hardly ever rained longer than a full hour up around the Divide in August. But on the other hand you got a lot of short, awesome thunderstorms back east, dumping a day's worth of rain in a short gully-washing fit.

It was more unsettling to living critters capable of jumping when a lightning bolt sizzled and detonated close by. So it was mighty lucky they were moving the cows north along a hairpin on the west slope a few hours later when all hell busted loose, and Longarm was soaked to the skin by the time he could haul out his rain slicker and shrug it on. They'd just made it down amid scattered junipers by the time a bolt of lightning split one close to the trail. It made lots of cow hairs tingle while Saint Elmo's fire danced like ghostly glowworms off many a long wet horn. So knowing what was coming, and knowing a pony had feelings too, Longarm tethered the roan he'd been leading to a juniper so he and the buckskin he'd switched back to could go tear-assing after the herd as another bolt sizzled down to stampede the shit out of it.

There was no way to yell back and forth above the roar of wind, rain, and pounding hooves. But Longarm saw the others riding for Miss Edwina Chaffee knew their asses from their elbows as they fell into their proper positions, those on the downhill side spurring forward and those to the right, uphill, falling back. The luck in the way they'd been trailing lay in the natural right-hand swirling of cows in a blind panic. Some said herds south of the equator stampeded to the left, while others said cows were simply right-handed, like most folks. In either case, that was why it was best for a bullfighter to wave his cape from the bull's left if he wanted it to tear straight on by, or from its right if he wanted it to circle him as he twirled like a ballet sissy. Knowing that lightning-spooked cows were naturally inclined to veer off to their right, and knowing that that way was uphill and steep, Edwina Chaffe and her hands did all they could to encourage the leaders to go mountain climbing, dragging their bellies in some stretches, while everyone praised the Lord it was still daylight. For cows stampeded just plain suicidally after dark, but while it was bad enough when they could see you, a determined rider on a good pony could hope to sway, if not stop, the uphill progress of a wild-eyed cow.

As he forged upslope aboard his less skilled livery mount, Longarm spied Edwina way up ahead, long hair swishing wildly in the rain as she flashed her wet hat at the uphill leaders to . . . Jesus, not to *mill* them on a slope like this! Sweet Fanny Addams!

Longarm got his .44-40 out from under his slicker, and commenced to riddle the gray overcast above them with lead as he heeled his own mount up the steep grade. It didn't turn the stampeding herd to their left, away from him. Nothing this side of a locomotive was going to turn a stampeding herd to its left. But at least he was able to keep them headed straight uphill until Edwina, catching on, cut across the front of the climbing column to wave and cuss on the right side as well. Cows didn't climb hills as well as ponies. So the other riders were soon working with Longarm and their boss lady to keep them headed skyward, ever slower as the grade got ever steeper. And then the sun came back out, and you could hear the cows bawling and bitching as the rain let up and they began to wonder why they wanted to drag their bellies over all this wet green grass when it smelled so fresh and cool.

As the strung-out herd began to slow to a walk or even stop and graze, turning sideways on the steep grade, Longarm caught up with their owner to apologize. "I knew what you wanted us to do. But I didn't see how milling 'em on the side of a mountain was likely to hold 'em in one place."

Edwina put her limp brimmed hat back on, replying, "I saw why you were doing what you did as soon as you did it. I believe you rode up the Goodnight Loving Trail through Indian Country after all, Ginger. I just wasn't thinking straight when I tried to turn the leaders all the way around. On a grade like this they'd still be moving, whether they were dead or alive!"

Longarm nodded soberly. "I saw what was left after a herd spilled over a cliff in a thunderstorm one time. If I was you, I'd let 'em steady some and then drift 'em back down to the trail. You want to move stock away from where they've recently stampeded. It seems to be something in the air, or mayhaps on the grass, after a good scare."

She smiled wanly. "I'm not totally green about cows on somewhat flatter range. I didn't think we'd ever make it in to Holy Cross by nightfall anyway. With any luck we ought to be able to bed them somewhere snugger, with better grass and hopefully some water to keep them contented in place."

He agreed that sounded right. But of course it took far longer to manage. It was over an hour later when they had the still-spooky stock moving on along the trail. Longarm, mounted on the roan again, scouted ahead as they got into timber again, or in this case, tall stumps and some patches of burnt-out spruce. It was easy to read how someone had cut pit props, this far east of the new silver strike, in winter, when the snow was deep but handy for skidding timber. The burn looked older. There was thorn apple and chokecherry, even waist-high aspen shoots, along with the bluestem and onion grass growing in the fresh sunlight between the bare charred spruce boles. So the burn had likely been started by lightning or Indians during the less recent Ute troubles in these parts. The mountain nations, and the deer they hunted, liked aspen glades far more than old-growth spruce.

He rode on into a natural bowl where rainwater formed a grassy pool of better than a full acre. Night pickets riding the barren rim all around would find it easy to watch out for trouble both ways.

He rode back to rejoin Edwina, his spare mount, and the rest of the outfit, saying he'd found some sort of crater or sinkhole just right for a herd that size. When he mentioned trouble on the way through that burn, she surprised him by asking what he meant.

He waved a damp denim sleeve at the timbered slopes all around as he explained, "We may be hours from Holy Cross as cows may find comfortable, Miss Edwina. But who's to say about a butcher aiming to cut out the middle-folk, or a trash white who might just hunger for some long-horned rabbit steaks? It's none of my nevermind, but were you fixing to turn these cows over to somebody or start your own cow spread in or about Holy Cross?"

She explained she was delivering stock from her own larger herd east of Leadville to a mining company in Holy Cross. It would be up to them whether they wanted to keep the stock penned and trough-fed as they were butchered in turn for the miners' mess, or turned out to graze under mining company riders.

Longarm agreed the smart way would be a combined operation, with most grazing free grass, in summer at least, but raised more like beefstock in fenced meadows back East to save on the wages of a skilled cow crew. They both knew raising cows on a small scale in the high country worked best as a family-spread operation. You needed lots of cows, spread across miles of open range, to justify hiring top hands you didn't raise yourself. The more modest herd they'd been moving all day seemed about right for a settled-down stockman with a wife, enough daughters to help around the house, and maybe four or five half-grown boys to help with the stock and more serious chores.

As they rode along together, Edwina Chaffee confided she'd been raised on such a spread, but meant to hire her own damned household help when and if she ever cut some man in on her own bigger operation. She said, "I borrowed a more sensible grubstake from the banking side of the family after I was big enough to do it right on my own. Paid Cousin Jerome back in less'n the five years we'd shook on. You'd think I was bragging if I told you how many stockmen have proposed to take all my business worries off my poor little girlish mind, Ginger."

Longarm chuckled. "No, I wouldn't. But I promise not to propose, and I thank you for mentioning the way some gents act around gals with money, no offense."

As they reined in on the rim of that natural crater so her hands could gently drift the stock on down, as if grazing around that water hole was their own bovine notion, Longarm told Edwina about the wager Clara Drakmanton had made with Sky Kirby.

He saw great minds ran in the same channels when, without hesitation, the more rustic young businesswoman said, "There must be some catch to it. I didn't think much of that redhead's riding, but even a sidesaddle priss would surely just take the money and run. Why on earth would anyone ever buy a hole in the ground for a hundred thousand dollars if it was going to cost them an extra five-hundred-dollar bet?"

Longarm said, "Makes no sense to me neither. If I had a bet like that I'd just say no, take his thousand, and then go ahead and offer him the original price, in my own good time."

She said, "What if you thought the mine was really worth a lot more than a hundred thousand, and feared you'd miss out on it if you quibbled about your five hundred? We're talking mighty big money bet by high rollers I'd never be able to mess with."

"Neither the Morgans nor Vanderbilts roll just plain stupid," he said, thinking back to other stories about Sky Kirby as he mused half to himself, "He's made other bets as dumb, and lost at least some of 'em, without batting an eye."

By this time the herd was all down in the grassy bowl around the still waters. So they both drifted down as well, and Edwina decided on a patch of drier-looking grass as their campsite.

It was after sundown by the time they had their riding stock secured for the night, their bedding spread out across the dry grass and a cookfire going under some more serious grub.

Edwina said she didn't expect "Ginger" to ride his own turn as night guard. But he said he'd relieve one of the first shift as soon as he finished his supper. He never said he was too wound up with too much on his mind to turn in early. His mission for Billy Vail was his own beeswax, and the saddle tramp everyone seemed to take him for wouldn't have had all that much on his mind after a long day in the saddle.

He borrowed a more comfortable stock saddle nobody was using, together with its throw-rope and Remington saddle gun. The change in the shape of its tree might soothe some overworked patches of his rump, while a throw-rope could always come in handy with any bound and determined stray.

Edwina told him to borrow a spare bronc from her remuda that'd gotten off easy all day. It was a big stolid-looking Colorado Ranger, which was the Rocky Mountains' answer to both the Appaloosa and the Virginia Walker. It was speckled a lot like that Nez Percé breed of Indian pony, but was rangier and inclined to cover a lot of ground at a comfortable pace, like the Virginia Walker. Once he'd relieved the kid Jeff, Longarm was tempted to circle the rim above night camp faster than he knew he ought to. The unusual lay of the land had the night guard farther out from the herd than usual, and he didn't know whether he ought to sing as he circled or not. For as a more general rule, the cows were bedded closer for the night but out from night camp a ways. The notion of softly singing on guard after dark was designed to lull the cows, not to keep cowhands awake. A half-asleep cow tended to spook at unexpected night noises, and so, whether a night guard sang well or not, the familiar sound of his singing tended to drown out the hoot owls and skittering night sounds that could wake a cow up with a start.

Longarm decided he was too far out, with the herd too securely bedded in that well-watered hollow, to let fly his own versions of "Farther Along" or "Aura Lee." He'd been told more than once his baritone wasn't bad, but like lots of fair singers, he was inclined to doubt his own ability to carry a tune. That was one of the things helping the better singers. Fair singers were inclined to worry more about the tune than your average tone-deaf drunk, who'd sing at the drop of a hat without being asked.

Longarm silently lit a cheroot and let his rangy mount drift at its own pace, cropping grass, along the natural pathway along the crest of the rim. As the full moon ducked in and out of scattered but heavy clouds up yonder, it seemed as if someone was lighting up and blacking out the hollow to his left. One minute he saw each and every form down yonder, if only as a dark outline, and the next he'd have trouble even making out the reflecting pond in the center, as they let the camp-fire burn down to a ruby glow.

He was working on his second cheroot when he heard a long low rumble in the distance and muttered, "Aw, shit," recalling his own slicker was riding his own McClellan down by that fire.

He turned in the stock saddle he'd borrowed to rummage through the possibles lashed behind its higher cantle. He found a sticky nor'easter more by feel than sight despite its canary-yellow shade, but only left it loosely draped across his thighs while the night sky made up its mind. He was warm enough for now in his hickory shirt and denim jacket. Those oilcloth mail-order slickers got hot as hell once you put them on in anything warmer than a total blizzard.

Down below, Edwina Chaffee had obviously heard the threatening sky. For she was suddenly back in her own saddle, singing sort of sweetly, as she circled her cows closer. When Longarm heard another rider pick up on the same old song from the far side of the hollow, he took a deep breath and commenced to see if he could harmonize as the three of them serenaded the cows with "Leading Old Dan."

Nobody seemed to know who'd first made that one up, likely along the Goodnight Loving Trail from some of the words. As in the case of many real folk songs, the words of this one tended to shift as different singers, stuck for a line, grabbed a new one out of thin air. So Longarm just hummed along.

Nobody sang to cows with any heat, let alone war whoops and the comical Swiss yodels some vaudeville trick ropers fancied as the authentic sounds of the Wild West. Real cowhands might shout a cakewalk or rooster-crow a Texas border ditty while raising hell in town. But the closer you got to a dirge around cows, the more cows seemed to like it. Longarm had gotten good results with church hymns in his own cow-driving days.

So he was more than a tad surprised, and sort of pissed, when somewhere in the night he heard another voice bawling out:

There's thunder in the west, and it looks like rain,
But I'll screw her in a puddle, lest we never screw again,
Come and tie my pecker to a tree, to a tree,
Come and tie my pecker to a tree!

Then Longarm was riding in that direction fast, with the old Remington atop the slicker across his thighs, as he quietly but not too warmly called, "Ladies and a bedded herd up ahead, friend. So I'm asking you polite to simmer down!"

The dirty version of "Old Chisholm Trail" ceased and desisted in mid-verse. But the singer didn't sound too scared as he called back, "You all was singing, wasn't you?"

As Longarm drew closer, the moon came out some more to reveal a quartet of riders, their faces well shaded by the moonlit brims of their hats, all worn with a north range crush like Longarm's.

"We had us a stampede this afternoon," Lonngarm said, "and you boys must know how tough it can be to settle 'em back down amid these mountains."

The one who'd been making all the noise asked in a sneering tone how Longarm would like to settle down right where he was for keeps. Then one of the others snapped, "Drop it, Windy. The man just told you he was riding with a trail outfit, and we're looking for our just rewards in Holy Cross, not a fight nobody's paying for!"

Longarm kept his trigger finger where it was as he told them in a softer tone they were on the right trail for Holy Cross and asked if they wanted to drift in for some coffee before they rode on. The noisy one seemed to fancy the notion. But the quieter one who seemed to be giving the orders told Longarm, "We'd best go on around. We're in a hurry, and you're right about cows being tough to hold together in these hills."

So Longarm just stood his ground and wished them well as the four of them swung off through the burn more to the west. He didn't hear them talking about him because the one who brought the matter up waited until they were out of earshot before he announced, "Windy might have missed a hell of a brag back there, Fandango. I'm just about certain that was the one and original Longarm just now, all alone with an old rolling-block Remington to call his own!"

The not-so-young rider they still called The Fandango Kid just heaved a sigh and said, "Shit, why didn't you decide he was Jesse James so's we could share a reward as well as a brag? I noticed he looked something like that infernal federal deputy, in this light leastways. But the real Longarm packs a Winchester '73, not no single-shot saddle gun, and his saddle's said to be a McClellan, not no double-rigged roper. What in the hell would a famous lawman be doing up here with a herd of cows, even if that was him we just brushed with back yonder?"

The one called Windy grumbled, "I don't care whether he was somebody famous or not. He didn't like my singing and I mean to clean his plow when next we meet. He did say him and his outfit was headed for Holy Cross, didn't he?"

The Fandango Kid started to object, then shrugged. "I don't care if you want to murder him or marry up with him, as long as we do what we're going there to do first. But if any of you screw up before I've completed my deal with Sky Kirby, you can commend your poor souls to Jesus, for your dumb asses will belong to me!"

Chapter 9

The storm never came any closer. So Longarm got some sleep after everything quieted down. Then the gray jays and cross-beaks were cussing, and some angel of mercy had already put the coffee on. So Longarm knew Edwina Chaffee was planning on an early start, and just rolled out of his blankets to get on with it.

He naturally had to take a leak before he did anything else. So he hauled on his boots, donned his hat, jacket, and gunbelt, and rose and headed up the slope through the dew-wet grass. Nobody asked where he was going or to do what. The point of the Victorian prudishness later generations would laugh at was that you had to pretend you didn't notice a lot that was going on in a world of animal power and primitive plumbing. So neither Longarm nor Edwina said anything but "Morning" when they met just over the rim near the clump of thorn apple she'd just come out of.

After a hurried light breakfast they mounted up to head the herd on. The sun shone bright, but the west winds stayed cool and clammy. Some held mountain mornings in high summer smelled tangy, while not a few others thought they smelled as if some drunk had pissed all down the walls of a cedar closet. After they'd herded northwest a couple of hours they began to smell Holy Cross, if that was where all those chimneys were smoking and horses were shitting.

You herded beef *to* a town, but you seldom ran it *through* a town you ever intended to visit again. So once she'd scouted ahead, Edwina told them to swing her cows around town lower down and farther west

It wasn't easy, although Longarm could see it would have been way worse if they'd tried to hold the herd together on steeper slopes all speckled with tree stumps and riddled with try-holes. Nobody in town would have thanked them for all that cow shit washing downslope at them with the next rain either.

As they drove down into the northwest-trending valley the new settlement nestled in, Longarm was reminded more of Deadwood in its first summer than Leadville, even early on. The one jagged-ass main business street ran in line with the natural drainage, and was likely flooded, then swept clean, whenever it rained seriously. Nothing as imposing as carpenter's gothic, let alone brick, was likely to be built before at least one bigger mine commenced to show some real profit. So false-front frame, unpainted, was about as imposing as things got. Lesser structures, a lot of them painted canvas or tarpaper over frame, and others unpeeled log, occupied the slopes to either side on an unorganized grid of cinder paths and wooden stairways. A blue haze of woodsmoke hung above the rinky-dink settlement, and despite the hour, at least four pianos were going full blast, not in harmony.

Longarm knew why. Reporters writing about "roaring camps" tended to lay it on a mite, but if they didn't exactly roar, a lot of mining towns tended to drink, cuss, and play cards around the clock. That was simply because the mines were worked around the clock in staggered twelve-hour shifts, with work at the face never shutting down entirely and dirty-faced but well-paid men coming up out of the eternal night of mining at all hours, to wind down a ways before they hit the sack at most any time of the day or night.

Longarm knew that despite all their bitching and the secret skullduggery of the Knights of Labor, a hardrock miner made more than a coal miner, while both were paid far more than a crop worker or cowhand, making even a small mining settlement more tempting to whores, gamblers, and just plain crooks than a cow town the same size.

The holding pens of the mining syndicate Edwina was supplying with beef lay on the far side of the valley, of course. They'd likely had the prevailing winds in mind. There was just no way to avoid the smell of stockyards once you sited them anywhere near town. But the winter winds from the northwest didn't blow the stink through many open windows, while the winds in summer, when fresh air was a more desperate need, came more from the southwest.

The slopes downstream from Holy Cross had been logged bare as well, and strewn with cinders and trash. But at least they failed to slope as steeply, and there were only a few widely scattered try-holes. The lack of mining-claim stakes explained that. More fortunate prospectors often salvaged the stakes of abandoned claims.

By the time they'd negotiated the muddy creek running down the deep groove, some other riders who worked for the mining syndicate had come out to help, or get in the way. Some of them laughed when they heard a gal shouting orders. Others just ignored her and tried to herd strange cows their own way, with strange results. They'd have spilled the herd down the valley if there'd been more cows and fewer riders. Edwina was fit to bust as she accused them right out of trying to run some weight off her stock before the outfit they rode for had to settle up.

Longarm shared the respect her own riders felt for a pretty little thing who knew which end of a cow was which. So when he saw her arguing up ahead with a big grinning gent who didn't sit his pony worth shit, he handed the lead of his roan to a nearby Chaffee rider and heeled his buckskin to lope up to them.

As he reined in, the big company man's stupid grin faded some. Longarm was just as big, and had his Winchester riding thoughtfully across his thighs as he announced in a friendly but firm voice, "I want you company boys to back off and let us worry about herding this beef the rest of the way."

The spokesman for the mining syndicate, possibly self-appointed, grinned less certainly and replied, "Do tell? I thought this little lady was in charge of this here drive. I was just now telling her how we wanted to move 'em on up."

Longarm said, "You thought wrong. This beef don't belong to your outfit until they've been paid for on delivery. So I'm asking again for you to back off and let us deliver it. I don't mean to ask a third time half as polite."

"Don't gun him, Ginger, " Edwina sobbed in a dramatic tone, as if she thought Longarm was bluffing.

Longarm gently explained, "I don't want to. May have to. He's openly interfering with a cattle drive on a public right of way, and that gives us the same right to gun him as we'd have if he was a lobo, a Ute, or any other menace to our unimpeded progress. That's the law. You can look it up."

A couple of other company riders drifted in to join the obvious argument, a more sensible-looking one asking the bullyboy what was up. The big grinner said, "This tall drink of water just told me flat out that we wasn't welcome here. I was just fixing to tell him how we welcome unfriendly strangers here in Holy Cross, boys."

Young Jeff, the erstwhile drag rider, drifted in with his own Winchester Yellowboy across his chinked chaps. Before he could ask what was up, it was over. The more sensible company rider sighed and declared, "They never sent us to fight a war out here, pard. You do as you like. But we're headed back to the yards to let the boss make up his own mind, hear?"

Longarm was neither surprised nor disappointed when the asshole with the stupid grin rode after them.

Edwina Chaffee smiled radiantly at Longarm. "Thanks. If I live to be a hundred I'll never understand the way some men act."

Longarm chuckled. "That's only fair, Miss Edwina. I've been confounded all my life about the way some women act. I doubt I was as heroic as I might have looked just now. It's been my experience that men prone to bully women seldom have the sand in their craws to stand up to other men. That's likely what inspires 'em to pick on women in the first place."

She said, "Just the same, you may have made an enemy just now, and he as much as said this was his town. It might be safer if you were to let my boys and me worry about herding this beef on in and settling up with that moron's employers. For you can catch more flies with honey than with vinegar, and I doubt anyone will challenge me to a gunfight if I bat my girlish eyes and act helpless."

Longarm smiled sincerely. "I know exactly how helpless you can be, Miss Edwina Chaffee. You sort of remind me of another pretty little thing called Roping Sally, but that's a whole other story, and what say we head 'em on up the far side."

"I mean it, Ginger. You've been a lot of help up to now, but I might have handled that silly ape differently, and I still have to cope with his outfit, and well, didn't you say you were headed here to Holy Cross on your own business?"

Longarm nodded soberly. "Yep. Would have been there by now if I wasn't so prone to horn into the beeswax of other folks. It's been nice riding with you and I thank you for the beans, ma'am."

But as he swung his mount around to head back to fetch his spare, she spurred her own paint after him, falling in to his left as she panted, "I never meant for you to ride off angry, Ginger!"

To which he could only reply, because it was true, "I ain't sore. We met on the trail. We made a deal. The deal's been done. We got your beef to Holy Cross and like you just said, I got my own deeds to do in town. So, like *I* just said, thanks for the beans, and what else is there to say?"

"Well, we might at least have a drink or more together, once I've settled up with my buyers and my riders. You didn't say how long you meant to be in town. I could . . . sort of wait around if you wanted to ride back with . . . us."

It was tempting as hell. While he'd never seen her rope, she was built slimmer across the hips than poor Roping Sally, and *that* hard-riding gal had been almost too tight down yonder. But it might have been cruel to a nice gal, as well as unprofessional, to have her wait an indefinite time for an undecided outcome. So he let the chips fall as they might as he told her simply, "I can't say how long I may be in town or who might be riding back to Leadville with me. I won't know till I meet up with some folks who may or may not be in town, ma'am."

Being a woman, Edwina naturally put the worst possible meaning to his words, from her standpoint, and blurted out, "I might have known! I saw the way that sissy-riding redhead in green velvet was flirting with you up in the pass! The two of you made plans to meet here in town, right?"

Longarm didn't ride after her. He heeled his own mount the other way as he wistfully told it, "You may be just as well off with your balls cut off in childhood, old son. The rest of us can't live with 'em and we can't live without 'em. But there are times, like this, a man with a lick of sense just quits whilst he's ahead!"

He took back the lead of his spare with a sad smile of thanks to the kid who handed it over, and swung up the creek into town. They'd laid out their main street a tad to the north of the creek, so it ran along the back doors and under the shit houses of the business structures south of the muddy street. First things coming first, and seeing his two hired mounts had been ridden high, wide, and hard, he put them both in the best of the three town liveries, paying a scandalous boom-town price for their care and the storage of his riding gear and possibles.

He cradled his Winchester over one forearm, lest it tempt fate in that unlocked tack room at the livery, and strode the plank walk up the shady side of the street. He didn't do so because the morning sun was cruel at this altitude after a hard rain, but because the mine workers off duty after a night in the dank dark bowels of the Rockies tended to crowd the sunny side of the street, some sitting on the edge of the walk, just spitting and whittling, as they basked like lizards in the sun after a night under a wet rock.

There was no Western Union yet. That was why that informant had sent his wire from Leadville, and likely given his game away. It was too early to file a progress report in any case. So Longarm searched for and found the modest town lockup, a fairly stout log structure identified by a swinging sign that read, "Town Marshal."

He went on in. A portly gray-haired gent with a drinker's nose was drinking cough syrup, or so he said as he put the bottle back in a drawer of the desk he sat behind in the center of the one big room. Longarm had recognized the brand. It was none of his beeswax whether a man wanted to treat a cold with laudanum or not. Neither the grain alcohol nor the opium in that popular medication was illegal under current federal law. When Longarm introduced himself, the older lawman behind the desk declared he was the one and original Blackfoot Blake, the scourge of the Arapaho and exterminator of the Ute, but blood brother to the noble Blackfoot Nation.

Longarm said, "So I've heard. Siksika, Piegan, or Siha-Sapa?"

Blackfoot Blake blinked up owlishly. "What difference does it make? A Blackfoot is a Blackfoot, right?"

Longarm had been raised to treat his elders with respect, but there were times it wasn't easy. He could see how unlikely it was to be seriously adopted into *any* nation, red or white, when you didn't savvy a lick of its lingo. But he didn't dig deeper into whether Blackfoot Blake was a blood brother to the Algonquin-speaking folks who called themselves Siksika, Piegan, and such, or to the Lakota clans called Siha-Sapa, or Blackfeet, because of their own dark moccasins. The army had been confounded about that when they'd heard about all those Blackfoot Indians at Little Big Horn. Some Siksika up along the Canadian border had told Longarm they'd been confounded to learn of their great fight with the blue sleeves as well.

But Billy Vail hadn't sent him out scouting for any Indians, so Longarm explained how he hoped to catch up with One-Eyed Jack once he found a third party who'd been on intimate terms with both a dead barkeep and somebody else in town who was pretending to be innocent.

Blackfoot Blake shrugged hopelessly as Longarm hauled a bentwood chair closer to the desk and sat it astraddle. The town law told him, "We asked around. We being me and my two deputies. They're both up the street at the justice of the peace with some mining men who had too much to drink last night. I sure hate a man who can't hold his liquor. It's all that property damage as gives the rest of us a bad name!"

Longarm agreed no sensible drunk ever busted up the bar he drank at, and tried to steer the conversation back to the case he was on. "Nobody seems able to tell me who the dead man entrusted with that wire to Marshal Vail about One-Eyed Jack McBride."

Blake said, "That's on account nobody knows. We do know the dead man, Sean O'Hanlon, never left town himself. So that raises another point you and Billy Vail may not have thought through."

Longarm said, "We've already noticed McBride and O'Hanlon are both Irish names. So it's possible One-Eyed Jack confided in the wrong fellow Harp. But that's not saying McBride has to be using an Irish name right now."

Blake said, "It wouldn't matter all that much in Holy Cross. For all the hardrock furriners who ain't Cornish or Italian seem to be Irish. I don't know why real Americans are so afraid of hard work a mile down, do you?"

Longarm said, "Yep. I worked in some mine shafts when I first come West after the war. I used to think back on that when things got hard and tedious working cows at half the wages. But what's your point about Irish names? You figure the messenger who betrayed our informant was Irish as well?"

Blake reached in that drawer for more cough medicine as he heaved a vast sigh. "Don't matter if he was a Chinaman. What you and Billy Vail suspect just won't work."

Longarm waited tolerantly while the older man sipped more brain pickle. He figured Blake would tell him what he had in his mind as soon as he fogged it up some more.

Blake put the potent mixture away again as he sagely suggested, "The pal who sent that wire for O'Hanlon couldn't have been the one who told One-Eyed Jack about it. He'd have never sent word to Billy Vail about One-Eyed Jack being here in Holy Cross if he'd been a pal of One-Eyed Jack as well, right?"

Longarm said, "Wrong. I can see you ain't betrayed as many pals as some, no offense. Had that wire never gone through there'd have been no answer for the killer and his sneaky pal or pals to read. We know One-Eyed Jack is smarter than most when it comes to covering his own ass.

So I'd suspect the two-faced messenger went to him with Sean O'Hanlon's message right off. Then One-Eyed Jack told him to go on and send it, for more than one slick reason."

He got out a smoke, seeing he wasn't being offered one, and lit up without offering before he continued. "The killer had no way to make certain O'Hanlon hadn't already sent earlier messages, say by mail or another pal headed for Leadville. As I read his wire back in Denver, it could have been the first word on a federal want or just a follow-up. Not wanting to take that chance, One-Eyed Jack likely had the two-face act in fake good faith, bring back Billy Vail's own reply, and thus know better how to cope with the whole shebang."

Blackfoot Blake looked unconvinced, if he was still wide awake.

Longarm insisted, "Once they knew my office had nothing else to go on, who Billy Vail would be sending, and how long it would take Smiley and Dutch to get here, One-Eyed Jack was free to murder that barkeep, or have someone else murder him, at well-planned leisure. Old O'Hanlon got shot in the back in the dark with no witnesses. So naturally there was nothing for Smiley and Dutch to do, once they got here, but ask the usual questions, run in the usual circles, and give up."

"Then why did they send you?" asked Blackfoot Blake.

To which Longarm modestly replied, "I don't ask the usual questions and run in the usual circles. I ain't sure I ought to ask anyone anything official. Riding up this way with friendly cowhands, I seem to have given folks the impression I was some cowhand called Ginger. Might be interesting if I was to leave it that way, for now, and drift about asking less official. Have you ever noticed how even innocent gents tend to play their hands closer to their vests in the company of known lawmen?"

The older if less experienced lawman shrugged and said, "Nobody in town seemed willing to tell me shit when *I* asked who back-shot Sean O'Hanlon. But how in thunder do you propose to work in secret this close to your federal district court, Longarm? You're almost as famous as me all over Colorado!"

Longarm sighed. "I've asked that pesky Reporter Crawford not to put all them tales about me in the *Denver Post*. But he says he's stuck for local color, what with Hickok dead, Hardin in prison, and both Jesse and The Kid in hiding. That's what he calls gunplay, local color."

Then he blew a thoughtful smoke ring and added, "On the other hand, they ain't perfected that Ben Day process enough for real photographs of me to have appeared in the *Post* or *Rocky Mountain News* that often. And one old boy from West-by-God-Virginia walks, talks, and might even look the same as another. So if you don't tell nobody who I really am, I surely don't intend to."

Blake shrugged. "Sounds dumb to me, but suit yourself. I have no call to tell One-Eyed Jack you're in town. I don't even know who the son of a bitch is. So it might be fun to let him share in the total confusion. You want my deputies kept in the dark as well?"

Longarm blew another thoughtful smoke ring. There was more than one good reason to pay a courtesy call on the local law when you hit a strange town. Aside from avoiding grim mistakes when you had to throw down on a local citizen, local deputies could often back your play when you needed backing quickly.

But it wasn't hard to guess what experience it might take to be the underpaid deputy of a small-town lawman who felt no call to sort Siksika from Siha-Sapa. So Longarm muttered, "Like the old song suggests, farther along, we may know more about it. What do you say we neither fib nor advertise till I've been in town at least a few hours?"

Blackfoot Blake said he didn't care, and asked what Longarm meant to do next. The taller, younger, and far more sober lawman got back to his feet as he replied, "Better check me into some quarters for openers. I'd feel lighter on my feet if I could leave this rifle and some saddlebags I have back at the livery under lock and key. It ain't as if my spare socks, shaving kit, and such are great treasures, but it would be a bother to replace them at Denver prices, and you boys up this way pay as much as a dollar for a dozen apples!"

Blackfoot Blake agreed prices were a caution in mining country, where overpaid greenhorns didn't seem to know the value of American money. He got to his own feet, suggesting, "I can aim you at a fair hotel just up the way. It's run by a respectable army widow who's death on bugs and changes the bed linens betwixt guests."

So Longarm waited in the doorway, and they stepped out in the sunlight together as, somewhere, a church bell tolled ten A.M., which was later than Longarm had thought.

Old Blake waved expansively at a two story-frame across the way catty-corner. So that was the direction Longarm was looking, by good fortune, when gunsmoke blossomed off the false front of the one-story building next to the hotel and the rifle report and thud of a bullet into the raw meat hit Longarm's ears while he was swinging his saddle gun's muzzle up to meet the challenge.

He fired, levered the Winchester, and fired some more as Blackfoot Blake cried, "Shit. I've been shot!" Then Blake reeled away to find some place to sit and bleed. Longarm fired half his magazine blind into that false front, then heard somebody holler and fired again lower, to be rewarded with: "I give! For God's sake hold your fire!"

But Longarm had lived through that ruse as well in his time. So he fired again, and again, until his magazine was empty and nobody was making a sound from behind that false front.

He'd dropped behind a watering trough to reload by the time a young squirt with a copper badge and a drawn Schofield .45 came down the now-deserted walk, bawling like a sheep until old Blackfoot Blake, seated on a box in front of a barbershop with remarkable composure, called, "Not him, Ray. The cuss as shot me's up ahint that sign above the dry goods. Go see if we got him!"

So the kid deputy trotted across the deserted street as Longarm rose, moved over to the wounded town marshal, and laid the Winchester aside as he bent to unbutton the older man's bloody shirt, saying, "You aint bleeding so bad outside. Can you tell where the bullet lodged inside you?"

The old opium-sipper calmly answered, "Just above the heart. I don't know why I'm still breathing neither, but it is getting sort of tough, and what are them fireflies doing out in the street in broad-ass daylight?"

Longarm didn't answer as he soberly stared at the little blue-rimmed hole punched neatly through Blake's upper breastbone. The street and walks were crowding up again as others came back out of the holes they'd ducked into. Somebody declared, "Jesus H. Christ, someone shot old Blackfoot Blake!" Another shouted, "Whatever for? The old drunk ain't never done nothing to or for a living soul!"

Another older man wearing a rusty black suit and narrow-brimmed muley hat while packing a small black sawbones bag joined Longarm and the breast-shot Blake, observing, "We'd better lay him out flat while I see what can be done for him."

But Blake protested, "Don't you dare, Doc. I don't know how I know it, but I know that once I lay down and shut my eyes I ain't never going to be allowed to open 'em again and sit back up."

The local sawbones dropped to one knee and put a hand to Blake's old turkey neck, muttering, "You could be right,

Marshal. I've noticed gents in your position often seem to know what's coming. Would you like us to send for Father Donovan or Reverend Stern?"

The dying man began to sing, or croak, "Too sinful for Heaven, too ornery for Hell, what happened to Maggie, no mortal can tell!"

The kid deputy, Ray, came back to marvel, "You got him, Blackfoot! He wound up in that slot betwixt the hardware and hotel across the way full of pine splinters and lead!"

Blackfoot Blake chortled, "That'll learn 'em to mess with *this* child! I swear I don't know where all the new faces in town have been coming from, or what they're doing here, but I reckon I just showed one of 'em who's the *law* in Holy Cross!"

There came a murmur of admiration from the growing crowd, and some curious newcomer was told, "Old Blackfoot just shot it out with some outlaw and they both got kilt."

The sawbones repeated that he wanted to stretch his patient out on the planks. Longarm softly asked. "Can you save him, Doc?"

When the older man shook his head, Longarm said, "Then let the man die tall as he can manage whilst he greets Mister Death in as manly way as he wants."

Someone in the crowd declared, "By the Great Horned Spoon, he *is* a real man and I'm sorry if I ever called him anything less!"

There were other approving remarks. Longarm hoped the old drunk could still hear them. He rose, hefted his reloaded saddle gun, and crossed over to where Blake's other deputy and a smaller crowd had just hauled a shot-up stranger out into the dust and daylight.

The second kid deputy, this one called Wes, nodded at Longarm and said, "Ray told us you just fought on Blackfoot's side. Which one of you do you reckon put the fatal round in this son of a bitch?"

Longarm stared soberly down at the dusty blood-spattered figure in jeans and an old army shirt. He was mildly surprised to see the dead face didn't go with anyone he'd talked to since leaving Denver. The gunslick had been in his late twenties or early thirties. You could tell he'd been a gunslick by the tie-down buscadero gun rig and the blued-steel S&W double-action still in its holster, with its fist-fitting rosewood grips set for the side draw of a man who chose the time and place to go for broke with both heels planted in the professional's shooting stance. Another townsman had just hauled the gunman's fancy Creedmoor target rifle from the gap between the buildings. Longarm told the town deputy, since it was the town's beeswax, how the shit at their feet had fired through a chink in the board of the false front up yonder, adding, "He must have been perched for a time on the roof, Wes. You might be able to find somebody who noticed from any number of second-story windows all around."

Wes shrugged and said, "Anyone with nothing to hide should have come forward by now, Mister, ah . . . ?"

"They've been calling me Ginger lately," Longarm replied, not wanting to further confuse a so-called lawman who thought witnesses to a shootout were anxious to volunteer.

Wes said, "We'll prop this old boy up in the shade, and he'll likely keep long enough for everyone who cares to have a gander at him. He couldn't have just come out of nowheres to lurk on the rooftops in wait for poor old Blackfoot! How's the boss doing, by the way? Ray says he was hit pretty bad."

Longarm said, "Ray got that part right. I reckon they could have been after him, now that I study the scope sight on that Creedmoor Long Range. He sure ain't anybody *I've* ever brushed with before."

A young squirt in a butcher's apron, obviously more qualified than some to study on such matters, demanded, "How can you be sure, Ginger? Betwixt taking some pine planking and at least one bullet in the face before he fell on it, this old boy can't look exactly as his dear old mother might recall him."

Longarm nodded, but said, "I was in a war one time. You get so you can sort of put a man back together in your mind, once you've been required to scribble *some* damned name on his grave marker. You can see this one had brushy brows with a scar running through the right one, and that one gold tooth would be tough to forget as well, once you'd had a serious discussion with a cuss. But why don't we see if anything in his pockets wants to tell us who he was."

Longarm leaned his Winchester against the nearest wall before he hunkered down beside the unidentified cadaver. Wes said, "Hold on there, Ginger. Shouldn't we leave that to the coroner or . . . Hold on now. Who in blue blazes would be the senior lawman here now?"

Longarm started to say he was. Then he wondered why he'd want to say a dumb thing like that, and said instead, "Reckon it's a matter of seniority betwixt you and Ray, at least till the powers that be say different. Meanwhile, do you want to see if this rascal carried any damned identification if you don't want me pawing through his pockets?"

Young Wes dropped to one knee on the far side of the cadaver to gingerly start searching it, muttering, "Aw, hell, I wish they didn't piss their pants like that."

Longarm got back to his own feet and picked up his Winchester as he resisted an obvious observation. He just said he wanted to see how old Blackfoot was managing, and headed back across the street in the sunlight. It wasn't true they all shit their pants as well. But he'd often wondered why the army insisted on feeding troopers such a hearty breakfast just before they ordered them into battle.

Up in one of the windows overlooking the scene, the killer Longarm had been sent to find turned from the lace curtains as his confederate slipped in to announce, "They all think that glorified town drunk was the target. I still think that mysterious rifleman was after the other one."

One-Eyed Jack murmured, "You mean that tall drink of water they call Ginger?"

The confederate, who'd betrayed the late Sean O'Hanlon by showing his wire to One-Eyed Jack, said flatly, "Ginger my Aunt Fanny Addams. I still say that has to be the one and original Longarm from Marshal Billy Vail's outfit!"

One-Eye Jake turned thoughtfully back to the lace curtains as, across the way, the man they were talking about rejoined the others over the body of the late Blackfoot Blake.

One-Eyed Jack, who actually had two perfectly good eyes and the quick coyote wits of a born survivor, murmured, "I'll allow he fits the description if you'd care to recall that recent edition of the *Denver Post*. That was quite a story about the famous Longarm printed on their front page. Are you suggesting it was somebody else who captured Slippery Elmer Graves alive just a few days ago in Denver?"

His confederate replied just as surely, "Don't matter who that was. We know Billy Vail sent those other deputies up this way to search for you. Who's to say he'd just give up when he has someone good as Longarm on the same payroll?"

One-Eyed Jack said, "Me. I've made it my business to study up on the law and how she works. Billy Vail wanted Slippery Elmer too, and now that he's got him the arresting officer ain't about to chase all over creation before he appears at old Elmer's arraignment in that Denver District Court!"

The confederate didn't answer. One-Eyed Jack relented enough to growl, "Aw, don't blubber up and cry about it. Go ahead and check out that Ginger gent if you like. You know I hate noise and like to play my cards close to my vest. But hell, we'll kill him fast should you turn out to be right about him!"

Chapter 10

It was well past noon before Longarm felt free to check into that hotel he'd been headed for in the first place. Those few in Holy Cross who called him anything were still calling him Ginger. Nobody paid all that much heed to a stranger who kept his mouth shut and his ears open while a heap of others were holding forth in a learned way.

By the time they had the late Blackfoot Blake in the undertaker's cellar, with his dead killer reposing on a sloping door there too, they'd worked out a dozen versions of the epic gunfight, not a one of them accurate, but old Blackfoot Blake would have been as pleased with any of them. For how often had even Wild Bill managed to fight, and win, with a bullet in his heart?

Longarm was saved having to sign a false name when the no-longer-young but still handsome Widow Lawford of "Lawford's Last Post" met him in her small lobby and gushed, "Oh, do come right in, Mister . . . Ginger, isn't it? I saw the whole thing from an upstairs window, and you'll never know how pleased with you I was when I heard you'd given all the credit to poor old Marshal Blake! Someone said the two of you were headed over here to hire a room when that killer opened up on you next door?"

Longarm nodded soberly. "Yes, ma'am. It was me in the market for a room. You say you saw that rascal on the roof open up with that fancy Creedmoor?"

The lavender-haired lady in the blue dress shook her head. "I've a blank wall facing that way, which the rascal on the roof doubtless noticed. But I naturally heard the shot, ran to a front window, and saw it was you, not Marshal Blake, shooting back. He was just sitting there with his own side arm never drawn. Yet you never said anything when everyone assumed he'd defended himself so bravely?"

Longarm shrugged. "He was brave as most could manage, considering he'd been struck fatally by the first shot. I had no call to rob him of such glory as a man might rate while staring Mister Death in the eye and singing him a comical song."

The sweet lady dimpled at him and declared he'd still been a young gentleman. When he asked what she wanted for a room, she told him he could have one close to the bath upstairs for six bits a night. She added, "I know that sounds dear, but my expenses up here where everything comes in by mule train are outrageous."

He said six bits sounded more than fair, and added he had a roll and saddlebags to fetch from the livery as well. But she suggested they settle up first so she could give him his key and let him come and go as he pleased.

He gave her the seventy-five cents, and she found him the key with his room number on the hard-rubber tag. He said he'd take her word the room was up there, and repeated what Blackfoot Blake had told him about bugs and clean linen over this way. She sighed and said she was sorry now about some of the things she might have said in the past about an old man with a bit of a drinking problem.

As she followed Longarm back to her front door she explained, "My late husband and me were once stationed at Fort Benton, and Blake would go on and on about Indians he knew nothing about."

Longarm said he'd noticed that, ticked his hat brim to her, and legged it back to the livery without incident. He was on his way back with his saddle gun in one hand and his possibles braced on a hip by the other when he met up, again, with that grinning company rider from earlier that morning. The bullyboy had obviously washed a light breakfast down with fifty-proof redeye. For his grin seemed even sillier when he joshed, "Heard you was there when the marshal shot it out with some other saddle tramp, Ginger. You sure the two of you wasn't in on it together?"

Longarm asked pleasantly enough how the beef sale had gone off to the northwest.

The mining syndicate rider, caught off balance, blinked and said, "I reckon the Chaffee outfit got a fair price. They rode off with neither their cows nor a declaration of war. I was talking to you about your own annoying habits, Ginger. What makes you act as if you think you're better than me?"

Longarm swung the muzzle of his Winchester up to brace the far unfriendly end atop the pest's belt buckle, which was pressed tight against his gut, as he cocked the hammer and softly replied, "Shit, your average yard dog is better than you, and one hell of a heap smarter. I told you before not to fuck with me, and there you stand like a big-ass bird with your mouth still flapping foolish at a grown man with three guns. I know you can only see two. But I carry a derringer tucked away for emergencies as well. Is this an emergency, you dumb shit?"

The bullyboy's grin faded as he whimpered, "Jesus H. Christ! Nobody said nothing about no gunfight, Ginger!"

Longarm growled, "What else do you expect a man packing his guns in plain sight to fight with, his feet? They say the first man shot dead by Henry McCarty or Billy the Kid was a blacksmith called Frank Cahill. Some say he was colored while others say he was white. But in either case he took to rawhiding the kid and daring him to fight, even though anyone could see the kid was way smaller and packing a six-gun. So Cahill must have been as dumb as you."

Their tense discussion had not gone unrecorded in a town already stirred up by a recent shooting. So the town deputy called Wes came down the walk to call out, "Hold your fire, Ginger. That's Hyena Harris from Amalgamated Minerals, and though I know he's a pain in the ass, he has some pals who'd take it serious if you gut-shot him."

Longarm nodded at the lout he had the drop on and said, "I still don't mean to go through this bullshit every time we meet, Hyena. I got more important things than you on my mind, and if you get in my way again I'll swat you like a fly and just get on with it, no matter how many pals you've got. Do we understand one another better now?"

Hyena Harris was too green around the gills to manage much more than an agreeable croak. So Longarm removed the gun muzzle from his gut and said, "*Bueno*. You'd better git now."

Harris started to say something else. But when Longarm repeated, "*Git!*" the bully turned and strode off suddenly, not looking back.

Wes chuckled. "I told 'em on the town council you'd struck me as a gent who could handle hisself in a tight corner. I don't suppose you'd like to hear what they're offering any man who'd be willing to try and fill Blackfoot Blake's boots and wear his tin star?"

Longarm chuckled at the picture. "Not hardly. Why can't you or young Ray take the job?"

Wes sighed. "I already asked 'em that. They say we look too young and innocent. They say *looking* like a hardcase lawman is half the battle, because lots of troublemakers don't want trouble with a gent who resembles the daddy who used to whip 'em regular."

Longarm said, "Makes sense. I've known a few younger-looking lawmen who managed well enough. But it's true they might not have had as many fights if they'd looked meaner. We all know the army hates to promote a company clerk to first sergeant before he's starting to get stout and gray. Recruits are more inclined to obey a bulldog than a terrier, no matter how tough either might be."

Wes walked beside him as far as the hotel, trying to get him to change his mind. The younger and greener lawman said,"They're sort of worried at the town council, Ginger. A man who looked the part better could doubtless get them to pay more than they paid Blackfoot. There's all sorts of sinister strangers crowding into Holy Cross, now that word's got out about some mines actually producing. Before he was gunned this morning, Blackfoot told us he'd gotten wanted fliers fitting more than one new face in town. Me and Ray ain't the only ones who suspicion that was why they gunned Blackfoot. Somebody might have been worried he was getting warm!"

Longarm started to dismiss this. But upon reflection he saw it was possible he'd been bragging to himself about the intended target of that long-range Creedmoor. The range the rascal had fired from had been close. Blake had been hit almost smack in the heart as well. So yep, that might explain why the killer had been such a total stranger. He might have known Blake, and vice versa, far better!

They'd just parted friendly in front of the hardware next to his hotel when he saw Clara Drakmanton and Sky Kirby sail out the hotel entrance. The handsome Clara had changed to a lighter tan habit of shantung silk, but there was no mistaking the auburn hair pinned up under that straw boater. Sky Kirby still wore his dark frock coat and matching slouch hat, although he looked a tad less dusty and didn't need a shave. Neither of them seemed to notice Longarm as they swept on to the surrey waiting out front. Longarm idly wondered where the high roller had hired it, along with that matched team, this side of the pass. The high roller helped the redhead aboard, and they drove off before Longarm could ask.

Inside Lawford's Last Post, the older but softer Widow Lawford was feather-dusting an already shiny rubber plant. When she offered to show him up to his room, he almost said he could find his own way. Then he had a better notion, and let her precede him up the steps as he asked her in a desperately casual voice how long Sky Kirby and Miss Clara had been staying there.

Without turning on the stairs she told him, "I don't know where that sporting gentleman may be staying. Miss Drakmanton checked in last night. Later than I'd have let her had she wanted to check in with any man with a different last name. I wasn't paying that much attention just now, but I think they said something about riding up the valley to look over some mining claim. You say you know them, ah, Ginger?"

Longarm replied, "Met them up around the pass yesterday. Can't say I know either one of 'em all that well. She did say something about some mining claim, though. Don't suppose she told you what she did when she wasn't digging for silver?"

The widow said, "She told me she owned her own rental properties and ran a real-estate agency in Pueblo. She gave me no reasons to doubt her."

Then they were on the second floor and she was opening a door with her own passkey as she waved at another door across the way and told him, "That's the bath. We like to keep up to date over here on the western slope, but I can't promise there's any hot water left at this late hour. My hired help stokes the boilers twice a day. Before dawn and just before supper time."

Longarm agreed early morns and evenings were the civilized times to take a serious bath, and held his own council on the way his own crotch was itching after a day in the saddle, a night with his pants left on, and not even a whore-bath since. As he admired the sunny room and draped his possibles over the foot of the bed, the army widow said, "You were in the cavalry when you were in the service, weren't you?"

He leaned his Winchester in a corner near the head of the bed as he quietly replied, "I don't remember much about the war, being sort of young and foolish at the time. Most of my Indian scouting for the War Department out this way has been civilian status, ma'am."

She nodded, but insisted, "Once a cavalry rider always a cavalry rider. I could tell by the way you wear that hat, and the way you fired your rifle from the hip before."

He shrugged and modestly replied, "A man has to set his hat on his head one way or the other, and to tell the truth, they issued old seven-shot Spencers during the last Shoshone scare and told everyone but me how lucky they were to have 'em. I was just as glad I packed a Winchester '73 when it turned out the Indian Agency had issued a mess of Henry repeaters to Buffalo Horn's band a few days before they jumped the reserve. I reckon everybody fires most any sort of rifle about the same, from the hip, ma'am."

She shook her lavender head wistfully. "You walk as tall and relaxed as a soldier blue I once knew too. You remind me so much of each other I could cry. You see, he was riding with Benteen at Little Big Horn and never made it as far as Reno's Hill."

Longarm removed his hat as he answered, "Marshal Blake told me your husband was no longer with us, ma'am."

She looked surprised, almost laughed, and declared, "Oh, Donald? He wasn't killed at Little Big Horn. He died of the yellow jack down at Fort Hood the summer before last. My . . . soldier blue was somebody I met when *I* was young and foolish."

Longarm didn't ask how young. He'd already guessed at how foolish. For Little Big Horn had been less than two army hitches back, and she'd doubtless been tinting her hair longer than that. The regular army was sure a caution when it came to running up bar tabs at the officers club and screwing one another's wives, assuming the cuss she still felt so wistful about had been an officer. Lots of army wives seemed to fancy the forbidden fruit from the ranks, or maybe they just found it easier to get away with a roll in the hay with an enlisted stable hand. That colonel's lady who'd damn near raped him that time in a hayloft had allowed she was being democratic with her old ring-dang-do. He'd only found out later how freely she'd shared it with damn near her husband's entire regiment.

The widow finally said something about other chores downstairs and left him to his own devices. The first thing he did was duck across to the hall bath and test the hot tap of the zinc-lined tub he found there. The water came out about as warm as piss but a lot nicer-smelling. So he put the stopper in and let it run as he ducked back across the hall to gather up a fresh shirt and underdrawers along with a change of socks, a cake of naphtha soap, and a terry-cloth towel from his saddlebags. Then he went back to the bath, bolted the door, and stripped down to climb in while the water was still shallow but rising. He could take tepid water better if he let it sort of sneak up his soapy hide.

Given more time and hotter water, Longarm was inclined to soak after soaping his balls. But Billy Vail hadn't sent him up this way to soak, and it didn't feel so grand in any case. So once he'd made the tub water dirtier than his hide he climbed out, rubbed himself dry, and got dressed most of the way. He hadn't noticed till he started to put it on, but he'd gone and packed a dirty shirt in his hurry to catch that train to Leadville.

He didn't cuss that hard, recalling he'd packed a couple of other shirts as well. He just hauled on his jeans and boots over the fresh socks and underwear, balled the two soiled shirts together, and put his gun back on to recross the hall hatless and naked from the waist up. From the way Widow

Lawford gasped all goggle-eyed when he burst in on her in his room, you'd have thought he'd come in waving his naked dong at her.

He said, "I'm sorry, ma'am. I thought I'd hired this room to be alone in."

She gestured weakly at the tray of coffee and cake on the dressing table, stammering, "I thought you could use some refreshments. When I knocked and nobody answered, I assumed you were across the hall."

Longarm nodded. "You assumed right, ma'am. I just had a bath, and now I mean to find me a clean shirt, both of these needing soap and water for themselves."

He expected her to leave as he moved around her to get at the saddlebags. As she went on gawking at the hairs on his chest, he smiled uncertainly and murmured, "Ma'am?"

She flushed and stammered, "Forgive me for staring. It's just that you seem so tall and slender when you're fully dressed, yet so . . . Grecian with your shirt off."

He nodded. "You have me at a disadvantage then. I can't tell how Greek you look under that buttoned-up bodice."

She blushed like a lavender-headed rose and called him a fresh young thing, adding he was young enough to be her son as she crawfished out the door and slammed it shut.

He chuckled, carried the tray over to the bed table by the open window, and sat on the bed to inhale the coffee and cake.

Both were swell and he hadn't eaten since the crack of dawn. So the cake was soon gone, and it was a good thing she'd brought the pot along with the cup. The sugar and goat's milk he didn't bother with. He lit a cheroot as well, sitting by the window as he worked on what he wanted to do next.

Out front, the main street had come back to life and was as busy as most cow towns on a Saturday night. He knew it felt sort of like Saturday night to a mining man who'd been working the night before in the even deeper darkness underground. Others down yonder didn't put in any honest work at any particular hour, if they could avoid it. He could tell by their outfits that half the crowd or more had never been down a mineshaft in their lives. It was a sad fact of frontier economics that there was more money to be made off miners than down in a mine. With any luck, things would simmer down a mite as Holy Cross got over its early growing pains, if it didn't die on top of a bunch of abandoned claims and bottomed-out mines. Meanwhile, there were more quick-buck artists than mine workers or even honest merchants, barbers, barkeeps, and such.

Somewhere in the neighborhood of his hotel a rinky-tink piano was going full blast in a way that somehow made it feel late at night in spite of the bright sunlight. Longarm perked up when the piano player hit a false note. But as he or she picked up the tune again, Longarm knew it couldn't be his old pal Miss Red Robin.

That was sort of sad in a way. For the awful pianist but great lay he'd often met in boom towns such as Holy Cross might have been able to help him out. Someone who knew the town better and might not tell the whole town who he was could give a lawman a leg up on One-Eyed Jack. A little slap and tickle with the voluptuous Red Robin wouldn't kill a man who hadn't been getting much lately either.

He finished the last cup of coffee, gripped his cheroot between bared teeth, and told himself to cut that out. It was time he put his shirt and hat on to go scouting, never mind working up a pointless hard-on for a gal who wasn't even in town!

He snubbed out the smoked-down cheroot on the window-sill and got back to his feet to rummage for that blamed shirt. So just as he was moving one way, bare from the belt buckle up, the room door opened and the lavender-haired Widow Lawford came in from the hall, wrapped in a floral kimono and blushing even harder as she opened it wide and demanded in a shyly defiant tone, "So go ahead and look!"

He did. Most men would have. Ben Franklin had been right about trees and women frosting from the top. Her perky cup-cake breasts were still as firm as a much younger woman's, and who cared if a lady sported a triangle of iron-gray fuzz between her smooth ivory belly and well-turned thighs when both the belly and thighs looked so young and frisky!

She primly shut her kimono again as she sassed, "There. I hope you're satisfied!"

To which he could only reply, "Not hardly!" Then he took her in his bare arms and reeled her in for a hungry kiss.

She kissed back as ravenously at first. But then, as he started to move them both toward the bed, she turned her lips from his to protest, "Stop it! What do you think you're doing? Can't you take a joke? I was only having sport with you, you silly boy!"

He fell across the mattress with her, and ran his free hand down between her thighs as her kimono fell open again. She tried to cross her legs, and then rubbed them briskly together on either side of his questing fist as she protested, "Unhand me, sir! Is this any way to treat a poor old widow! You ought to be ashamed of yourself, you naughty boy!"

Then he was French-kissing her, so she had little more to say until he'd shucked his gunbelt, got the top of his jeans out of the way, and rolled atop her with a suddenly raging erection.

As if she had eyes down yonder, his kimono-clad landlady threw her thighs and further shyness to the four winds, moaning in either pleasure, surprise, or both, as he drove into her to the hilt and felt her bite down hard with her moist warm innards. But even as they commenced to screw like old pals, both moving with considerable skill, she sobbed, "Oh, no, I never meant my little tease to go so far, and whatever must you think of me now?"

He said, "I think you'd feel even better belly to belly if we got rid of your kimono and my boots and jeans!"

She protested it was broad daylight, and told him this whole situation made her feel so wicked as he stripped them both all the way and slid a pillow under her naked rump before he mounted up again. He only had to move in her a couple of thrusts at that swell angle before she moaned, "Oh, Lord, you were right! It does feel lovely this way and I can't help myself as you screw me, screw me, screw me till I come a hundred times!"

In point of fact, Longarm only managed to come three times before he just had to take a break and light another smoke. She bragged she'd climaxed five times as she snuggled close with her lavender hair unbound across his bare chest, resting her head on his naked shoulder, playing with the hairs below his belly button.

When he allowed he'd try to catch up with her as soon as he got his second wind, she demurely asked, "Haven't you had enough of my poor old wrinkled flesh by now, you naughty boy? I swear I don't know what came over me just now, or how I'll ever face you again as soon as this mad passion cools! You must think I'm just a dirty old bawd after the way I just carried on!"

He kissed her and said soothingly, "We ain't through carrying on, and you ain't no more dirty than the rest of us, ma'am."

She giggled and said, "They used to call me Beverly, Ginger."

He blew a smoke ring up through the shaft of dusty sunlight a yard or so above the bed. "Like I was saying, Bev, a human body that ain't been laid for a while, be it male or female, gets to confounding its usually more sensible parts with thoughts they say Queen Victoria don't approve of."

He gripped his smoke with his teeth and moved her hand farther down to grip his flaccid pecker right as he mused on.

"But come to study on it, I doubt even a queen could have that many kids by way of immaculate conception. The late Prince Albert was a tall drink of water, and she's always been a little butterball. So it's sort of amusing to picture the two of 'em going at it hot and heavy in the Windsor Castle with all them ancestors and suits of armor watching."

Beverly Lawford laughed incredulously and said, "I don't think it's proper to picture Queen Victoria doing anything that shocking!"

He shrugged and said, "I said I found the picture amusing, not all that shocking. How else might she and old Albert have wound up the grandparents of Europe? Did you know the future kings of England, Germany, and Russia are all going to be old Victoria's grandsons? I swear, she and Albert must have screwed like rabbits in their day. For even when you want to, you don't get a kid each and every time you rub your old ring-dang-dos together, you know."

She murmured, "Indeed I do. I don't have to worry about that anymore, thank God. I don't know why I never had any children before my change of life. Lord knows it wasn't for lack of trying and . . . Oh, dear, I never meant I had lovers on the side when my husband was still alive. Not many lovers, at any rate. Why am I speaking so freely to you, Ginger?"

Longarm said, "It's a gift I have. Sometimes I wish I didn't. A lady I met a spell back said there was something about the way I didn't seem shocked that inspired her to confess some things from her past even *she* found shocking. I can't say I was shocked. But it did sort of spoil the mystery when she allowed it had been her dear old dad who'd taught her to suck so swell."

The obviously experienced Beverly gasped and declared, "Such a confession would tend to rob an affair of some romance. I think I may just let you guess who taught me how to pleasure a man that way."

100

Longarm didn't care as she kissed her way down his belly with his shaft firmly gripped in her hand, and licked the head to inspire another erection with her pursed lips sliding up and down an astounding distance. He knew the lucky bastard had enjoyed it before he'd been killed by Lakota, yellow jack, or whatever. He was pretty sure she'd had a heap of lovers in her day. Just as he was sure none of them had been around too recently. For nobody who could get at anything that skilled and sweet would be likely to leave it alone.

He knew she was even hornier than he was when she suddenly took her lips from his fresh wet erection and swung around to impale her naked crotch on it, moving on top to surprise him another delightful way as she threw her head back, eyes closed, and bounced like hell, sobbing, "I don't care if I'm a dirty old lady getting ravaged by a saddle tramp in broad daylight! I needed this, and it feels so good with me controlling its lovely deep thrusts!"

Longarm was too polite to ask who might be ravaging whom. So he just lay back and enjoyed it as he ravaged the hell out of her without having to move at all.

Chapter 11

Longarm couldn't see why old Bev felt so shy after he'd come in her doggy-style with both of them watching in the mirror. For it had been her suggestion, as well as a heap of fun. But once the sweet if dirty old lady had run off to hide somewhere, Longarm had another bath, quicker, in colder water, and found the streets a tad less crowded by the time he was finally back out on them.

By now it was late afternoon, with no shifts moving to or from the mines in the near future. But pianos were still tinkling and glasses were still clinking as he passed saloon doors on his way to the saloon he was most interested in.

Thanks to all that time on the train and trail with nothing else to read, Longarm didn't need to consult his notes to remember the late Sean O'Hanlon had tended bar and been shot near the shithouse of the Lucky Seven Saloon across from the town corral and smithy. There was nobody playing the piano against the back wall, and more than half the tables and most of the bar seemed deserted at that hour. Longarm bellied up to one empty end of the bar and told the wiry balding barkeep he'd try some of that ice-cold draft they advertised out front.

The schooner he got for his nickel wasn't quite as big and

not nearly as cold as he'd been led to expect. He knew most such brags were based on the draft barrels being stored below in dirt-floored cellars and kept deliberately damp and sort of cool by occasional pails of pump water. He told the barkeep it was about time somebody pissed down the cellar steps, keeping his tone light as he said he'd heard damp wood and dirt dried out faster at this altitude. He didn't really give a shit. But when the barkeep shrugged and allowed he only worked there, it gave Longarm the chance to say, "So I've noticed. Wasn't there another gent named Sean Something behind that bar the last time I rode through, say two weeks ago?"

The new barkeep replied just as easily, "Sean O'Hanlon. He got killed since then. Happened out back just last week. Nobody can say who must have been laying for him in the dark that night, but somebody surely was. Blew him off his feet with a shot in the back and pumped four more in him as he lay there dying!"

Longarm whistled, leaving the change from his quarter on the damp mock-mahogany as he sipped some suds before saying, "I'd heard there'd been a recent shooting over this way. Hadn't connected it to good old Sean till now, though. Who'd want to gun a harmless cuss like him? I thought everybody liked him."

The dead man's replacement nodded. "He was a good old boy. Had lots of friends, but as the late Blackfoot Blake said at the time, it only takes one enemy."

Mention of the more recent death of their town marshal seemed to inspire some conversation at a nearby table. Longarm sipped more suds and told the barkeep, "Too bad O'Hanlon didn't take one of his real pals with him that night. Who was that one pal he spent a heap of time with after hours? Jim, Jack, something like that?"

The barkeep thought and then decided, "You might mean Trevor Crockett. Him and Sean were sort of close, and old Trev's a Cousin Jack, not a real American called Jack."

Longarm said cautiously, "I do think his pal had a Cornish way of talking, now that you mention it. Them hardrock gents from the tin mines of Cornwall all talk that same sort of comical way. You say old Trev works the day shift, leaving him with heaps of free time late at night?"

Before the barkeep could answer, one of the townsmen seated at that nearby table rose to come over and say, "This cowboy's having his next one on us, Kev." Then he smiled at Longarm. "Ain't you the one calt Ginger? The pal who backed poor Blackfoot's play as he shot it out with them outlaws this morning?"

Longarm said, "I was there when he got the one who put a rifle bullet through his brave old heart. This is the first I heard about outlaws. Are you saying they've identified that cuss propped up on that cellar door?"

Since he didn't seem to be moving from the bar, the two others who'd been seated at that table rose to join them as the friendlier one nodded. "Well, sure they have. Half a dozen folks around town recognized him as the road agent who held up that stage over on the Lyons run more than once. Don't never get killed this close to the scenes of your crimes if you don't want nobody to notify your next of kin!"

Another of the trio volunteered, "He was a Fremont County boy gone wrong. Name was Penn, Wrenn, or something like that. Hailed from an honest homesteading family just outside Coal Creek, but he must have felt too proud for honest toil."

The one who'd offered to buy said, "There were three of 'em as held up all them stages. We figure they must have figured old Blackfoot had figured they were in town. So they decided to gun him before he could figure out where they was holed up here in Holy Cross."

The other volunteer shook his head and opined, "They're long gone by this time. Ain't no place in this valley a man could hide after gunning such a popular lawman. But they won't get far with Wes and Ray leading posses two ways after 'em."

Longarm cocked a brow. "Then both your paid-up lawmen are out of town right now?"

The townsman seemed unconcerned as he nodded. "One posse went back over the pass in case the outlaws headed that way, and the other down the trail into the recent Ute reserves in case they're streaking for Grand Junction and the Mormon Delta. Young Penn wasn't no Mormon, but who's to say what his pals might have been."

Longarm said he had to go take a leak, which was true, but which killed other birds with the same squirt. It gave him a chance to add the two new names to his notebook before he forgot, and seeing he was back there alone in daytime, it gave him a chance to scout the scene of Sean O'Hanlon's murder.

He didn't find anything vital. The layout wasn't exactly as he'd pictured it in his head, but a cinder-paved backyard with the shithouse to the right instead of to the left as one stepped out the back door didn't tell him who'd been waiting out there in the dark, or even why.

For it was just as easy for one wanted man to ride out of town into mighty empty country as it would be for another. So they were going to feel silly as hell if One-Eyed Jack reappeared hundreds of miles away after they found out some drunk the barkeep had refused to serve had gunned O'Hanlon in a late-night snit!

Longarm had to drink that second beer and buy a round in turn. So when he left the Lucky Seven, he needed something more than old Beverly's coffee and cake in his gut before he drank anywhere else.

He found a chili parlor closer to his hotel, and ordered fried eggs atop a steak smothered in chili beans. When you ordered chili con carne you got the carne, or meat, ground up and mixed with the chili powder and beans. You got more meat to stick to your ribs if you could afford to order it his way.

Lawford's Last Post, across the way, still stood on the sunnier side of the street. So he had a much clearer view of that surrey pulling up to the front entrance than either Clara Drakmanton or Sky Kirby had of him, seated in the late afternoon shade by the open front of the chili parlor, as they got out in the sunlight.

He sipped coffee, just watching, as the high roller escorted the gal to the door, but parted from her there to trot back to his hired surrey and drive off fast as usual.

Longarm finished a cheroot as well as his coffee and pie. Then he got up, paid off, and ambled innocently across to the hotel to fetch that denim jacket he might just need after sundown.

There was a young Indian gal behind the counter as he came in. When she said her boss lady was indisposed and couldn't see anyone, but that she could hire him a room, Longarm waved his key tag at her and said, "Already got one, miss. I'll let myself in, and I sure hope Miss Beverly feels better soon. I take it she'd be having a lie-down in her own quarters out back?"

The pretty little Ute, or maybe Kimoho, said innocently that her boss lady had decided to spent the night with friends. Longarm didn't ask whether Bev was hiding out with male or female friends. It was enough that she was hiding out from *him*, bless her sweet old guilty bones.

He asked which room Miss Drakmanton might be in. The child behind the desk didn't hesitate to say the lady from Pueblo was checked in right next to him. So *that* was who'd used up all the hot water earlier.

He went on up, put on his jacket, and pawed through the recent fliers in a saddlebag until he found mention of a federal want on the person or persons stopping that mail stage on the far side of the Divide. There were no names on the all-points Denver had gotten. The Leadville or Lake

County law had likely gotten the more recent line on that kid from Coal Creek.

He waited by his own door until, sure enough, he heard the door across the way slam shut, and popped out in the hall just in time to catch Clara Drakmanton coming out of the bath. Her kimono was a jade-green brocade, and she'd wrapped her auburn hair in a turban of white toweling. She gasped and declared, "Oh, you startled me, Ginger! I take it you're staying here too?"

He said, "Yep. But you're right about me tracking you down. I ain't trying to get fresh. I just wanted to know how you'd made out with that wild wager we were talking about."

She opened the door to the room next to his and waved him inside as she confided, "It was the fastest thousand dollars I ever made in my life. You were wrong about the floor being covered with silver dollars. All he had to show me, way up the slope, was a glorified gopher hole. He showed me some ore samples, he said, that I couldn't tell from plain old rocks. When he insisted it was a rich claim that only needed a little work to start producing, I told him to work as much as he wanted in such dusty surroundings, but that I was going back to Leadville. My only problem now is how I'm to get there. You don't know if that Chaffee outfit has left yet, do you?"

Longarm shook his head. "I can find out. If they can't keep you company over the Divide I might be able to find somebody else headed that way. You say that hole Sky showed you was dry and dusty? Not flooded or even ominously muddy?"

She insisted, "Dry as a mummy's belly button. Smelled sort of like a museum too. I can't go riding over the pass with just anybody, Ginger. You may not have noticed, but I'm riding a valuable mount and I'm not exactly deformed."

He assured her he'd never send her off in the company of gents less refined than himself, and added, "You don't want to head out this close to sundown in any case. Our landlady seems to be away for the evening, if she meant to serve any grub to begin with. But there's a fair beanery just across the way. So why don't you grab some grub and mayhaps a good night's sleep, and meanwhile I'll find out if anyone a pretty lady can trust is headed over the pass come morning. There's almost sure to be somebody."

He started to leave. She put a hand on his sleeve and asked him with a puzzled frown, "What do you think Sky Kirby's really up to? You're so right about not even the bigger outfits showing any profit by the time they send . . . What does stomped and washed mean?"

Longarm explained, "Ore as it comes out of the mountain is more than ninety percent worthless rock. You can crush it to powder and wash it as thin mud over riffles in hopes of floating the lighter grains off. The heavier grit you're left with ain't anywhere near fifty percent silver. But at least it's worth packing to more distant smelters, where it can be refined and sold as forty-pound ingots at a marginal profit. They still have to separate the silver, lead, iron, and such before they can use any of it right. So you call it high grade, crude pig, or pure as it makes its weary way to market."

She grimaced. "Sky must have thought I was a total idiot. All he had to show me, as I said, looked like common country rocks. Why do you suppose he felt so sure I'd bite?"

Longarm said he'd be proud to tell her if anything about the odd proposition made a lick of sense. When he asked if she'd packed along money, in case Sky had won, she shook her towel-wrapped head. "I even pay my grocery bills by check. You don't suppose he and his bunch could be after my fair white body, do you?"

Longarm asked if any of them had gotten fresh with her so far. When she allowed Sky Kirby had been a perfect gentleman, or hadn't laid hands on her at any rate, Longarm said, "He must have had something more sneaky in mind.

So like I said, you'd best stay close till sundown, and lock yourself in as soon as it gets dark. Meanwhile I'll see what else I can find out for us. I'll try to get back here by . . . What time do you usually turn in?"

She said, "Don't worry about me. I'll stay up. I know I'd never be able to close my eyes with all this confusion running around in my brain. Sky didn't even put up a real fight when I told him there was just no way I'd ever buy that mining claim. Do you think I will really find that easy thousand waiting for me when I get back to Leadville, Ginger? Sky Kirby would have to be a raving lunatic to honor a bet like that one!"

Longarm shrugged and said, "They say he's never welshed on a bet. But of course, that ain't saying he can't be a raving lunatic."

Chapter 12

Longarm didn't want to run into Hyena Harris again if it could be avoided. So he tried asking around the livery, and discovered Edwina and her riders had already headed back to Leadville after delivering that herd. It made him feel just a tad wistful. Old Edwina had been built mighty nice, and he was starting to recover from his unexpected pleasure with the lavender-haired Beverly.

By sundown he'd tracked down Trevor Crockett, without asking any questions that might alert a cuss with a guilty conscience to duck. The Cornish driller, as it turned out, was said to be trying to double his already handsome wages in the back room of the Hornsilver Saloon. So that was where Longarm headed next, and it was a good thing he hadn't showed up even two minutes later. For great card-playing minds seemed to run in the same channels, and he was sort of chagrined to be greeted in the tricky light out front with: "Custis Long, you old basser! What the hell are you doing in Holy Cross? Or should I just ask who you're after?"

He saw he was alone with the much smaller figure in the large cavalry hat just outside the swinging doors, grabbed her small elbow gently but firmly, and hauled Poker Alice up the other side of the rain barrel as he softly murmured,

"Howdy, Miss Alice. Let's you and me talk."

Poker Alice was a once-pretty woman of mysterious age and background who more than lived up to the brags of the better-known but partly self-invented Calamity Jane. The more petite Poker Alice wore fringed buckskins and smoked cigars, but never said how many men, red or white, she might have fought or fornicated. Longarm had never had to outdraw the tough old bat. So he couldn't say whether it was true she took that hogsleg on her hip dead seriously.

As he gently spun her to face him, Poker Alice asked, "What's got into you, old son? You're acting like you just seen a ghost."

Longarm said soberly, "You're the ghost, Miss Alice. What with one misunderstanding and another, a heap of folks here in Holy Cross seem to take me for a drifting hand called Ginger."

The sweet old hag grinned up at him. "Well, ain't you a sort of drifting cuss, Ginger?"

Longarm was tempted to kiss her. But he'd just found out some older women could take a man up on it, and Poker Alice could have used a bath. So he just said, "I always said you were smart. Seeing we're alone and you've been here longer, I'd like your opinions on some odd goings-on."

She said she'd only come over the pass from Leadville a few days earlier, inspired by talk about the high rolling with dice, cards, and mining claims that always went with a new strike. She said it seemed too early to say whether they were talking boom or bust. "We're about where Leadville was in '76, when the flash in the pan of placer gold gave way to more sensible talk of all that black sand in the riffles being worth something. You know how few make a go of mining in the end as claims good and bad are swapped for groceries or wagered as table stakes."

Longarm nodded. "I've heard you made out pretty good panning indoors with your poker deck, Miss Alice."

She shrugged. "I make a living at poker. It's less work than waiting on tables and more respectable than whoring. But if the truth would be known, both a whore and a waitress come out ahead at the end of the year. I play fair and deal from the top. So there are just a few damned rounds I win and some I really lose."

Longarm didn't ask how an honest poker player could come out ahead enough times to keep smoking nickel cigars. He knew Poker Alice was a shrewd judge of faces, and the true poker face was rarer than some poker players figured. He said, "If we were headed for the same back room, I'm interested in a driller called Trevor Crockett. Might you know him, Miss Alice?"

The old adventuress shrugged her buckskin-covered shoulders and replied, "Only to play cards with. He'd do better if he stuck to his drilling. Knows a face card from a trey, tries not to show it when he's holding four aces, but like I said, he's a mining man, not a poker player. What do you want him on?"

Longarm hesitated, decided honesty might be the best policy with a practicing mind reader, and replied, "Ain't sure he's done anything. They say he was close with that barkeep O'Hanlon someone back-shot a few nights ago."

Poker Alice nodded. "I heard about it. It wasn't me. I come over the pass about the time your pals, Smiley and Dutch, were up here asking about it. You can ask them if you want. Why do you suspect one of O'Hanlon's pals of killing him? Ain't it usually enemies?"

Longarm said, "Some pals are truer than others. I'm going to say you're fibbing if you repeat this, Miss Alice, but we've good reason to suspect O'Hanlon confided in a pal about the bounty on a certain wanted man."

Poker Alice nodded. "One-Eyed Jack. I told you Smiley and Dutch talked to me earlier. I don't know who or where that one might be. I wish I did. I could use the money, and I'd just tell the law direct. Why do you suppose that barkeep told all sorts of other folks he was on to a known killer? Sounds like a fool bragging on a night in bed with a married woman, albeit even riskier!"

Longarm started to say he'd narrowed it down to the unknown pal who'd been given that message to wire Billy Vail. But as soon as he studied on it, he followed the old gal's drift. It was true a lot of men shot their mouths off mighty dumb. As a lawman he knew all too well how many jealous husbands shot idiots who just had to brag to all the other men they knew. And almost as many outlaws wound up in prison because they didn't consider a stage stopped or a bank robbed until they'd told all the whores what they'd done.

He grimaced and said, "I wish you wasn't so smart about human nature, Miss Alice. Never having met the dead man, I just can't say how expansive he might have been. But sticking with targets I know of, might you know whether this Trevor Crockett makes occasional trips over the pass, mayhaps to pick up more dynamite caps back in Leadville?"

Poker Alice laughed lightly. "I only play cards with the cuss. I ain't sleeping with him. So don't ask me how free he'd be to come and go. Wouldn't they know better at the mine he works in?"

Longarm grinned down at her. "I'll ask. Sounds way quicker than asking sneaky questions over a card game. But what say we both go on in and have you introduce me to the boys as your long-lost son Ginger?"

She protested, "I ain't *that* old, you cruel young cuss. But I'd be proud to introduce you as an old boyfriend from Leadville."

He laughed, and they moved back toward the bat-wing door. But then they met two others dressed for a funeral, if not a more serious occasion, coming out, and Longarm was pretty sure at least one of them had been riding with Sky Kirby up around the pass.

He knew he was right when the other one ticked the brim of his black Stetson to the old lady and said, "Evening, Miss Alice. With your permission, Sky Kirby would like a few words in private with old Ginger here."

Poker Alice shot Longarm a worried look. He answered her unspoken question with: "I reckon I can handle it, Miss Alice. Sky said he might want to talk to me some more once we all got down here off the slopes."

Poker Alice nodded. "I'll expect you to rejoin me here in the back room with old Trevor and the others. If you don't I may come looking for you, hear?"

Longarm nodded, and Poker Alice pushed on inside. Longarm asked the two gents where they were going. One said, "Another back room in yet another saloon. Before you get your shit hot, Sky said to tell you he wasn't pissed at you no more."

Longarm didn't ask why, in that case, their boss had sent them out scouting for him. He was afraid they'd force things to a head before he knew where Sky Kirby was.

As it turned out, the high roller was dealing in the back room of that same Lucky Seven Saloon Longarm had visited earlier. The back room was a tad smaller than your average dining room, and all the action seemed to be at a big round table under a hanging oil lamp. There were six others seated at the table, and twice that many leaning against the walls all around to watch. Nobody there was dressed as casually as Longarm that evening. So it was tough to say how many were real mining men and how many were merchants, pimps, and such.

Longarm had been braced for some growling at least. So he was a tad confused when the dapper Sky Kirby greeted him like an old pal from the war, saying, "Howdy, Ginger. I've had good reason to feel more cheerful since last we met, and seeing you're packing a .44-40 and we heard about you taking part in that gunfight earlier this morning, I wanted to know if we were still pals."

Longarm shrugged and replied, "I like you as much as I ever did, and seldom throw down on anyone I don't have to. What are the table stakes, before I sit down?"

Sky Kirby nodded at the pot of red, white, and blue chips in the center of the table. "Chips start at ten dollars and go up to fifty and a hundred. You really want to sit in, Ginger?"

Longarm chuckled and replied, "Not just yet, thanks. You say you're all cheered up over something?"

Sky Kirby nodded. "Sold that mining claim you must have heard us talking about. I know you had your doubts. But Miss Clara Drakmanton took one look at my Silver Spoon claim and, just like I bet her, snapped it up for a mere one hundred grand. Wrote me a check on the spot this afternoon. So you see, you were wrong about my powers of persuasion, Ginger. Maybe next time you won't feel so certain!"

Longarm allowed Sky Kirby had him feeling mighty uncertain, and casually asked if Clara Drakmanton had headed back over the pass with that Chaffee outfit.

The high roller shrugged and said, "I reckon. She did say something about getting back to Leadville so's she could form her own syndicate to work the Silver Spoon proper. As I told you all up the trail, I'm not as interested as some in the mundane matters of a silver mine. That's how come I was willing to sell such a fine one so cheap after I won it at this very table not too long ago."

Another man at the famous table grumbled, "Are we going to brag about other games or play this one? I was there when you won the Silver Spoon off Pop Wagner, and I still say you won a rabbit hole."

Sky Kirby shrugged and started dealing as he smoothly observed, "Don't matter what I won, seeing I just sold it at a handsome profit. As Ginger here can tell you, the new owner is pretty too."

Longarm caught himself nodding. He could see now why the high roller had sent for him. The lying son of a bitch was trying to get him to verify a sudden windfall of a hundred grand. He was tempted to expose the asshole's little game. But then he decided to figure it out better first.

Unless Clara Drakmanton was lying, she'd not only refused to buy his fool claim, but had won one thousand off him too easy to be true. So all right, say a high roller needing credit in a new arena had figured it was worth one thousand to . . . do what?

Longarm found a space against the wall and lit a smoke in self-defense as he stared thoughtfully through the tobacco haze at the slicker cuss dealing. Most everyone there would have said he was dealing from the top. But Longarm had spent some time with a lady magician who'd shown him some other tricks when they hadn't been performing any in bed. So while Sky Kirby was good, damned good, Longarm had his doubts about some few of the cards skimming over the considerable pot to land neatly as trained butterflies in front of the other players. It seemed just as well the well-dressed but well-weathered player with his back to Longarm and an ivory-gripped Colt Lightning on one hip didn't have the same bird's-eye view of Sky Kirby's artistic hands. For he'd been dealt five cards in four suits and not a high card among them.

Hence Longarm was more than surprised when the betting commenced and the well-armed player with the piss-poor hand said he'd stay with his hand and raise.

Sky Kirby laughed and said, "You're my kind of player, Fandango," and shoved a stack of hundred dollar chips out from the pile in front of him. Longarm didn't say anything. More than one at the table did. They began to fold as the man known as Fandango raised a second time and the pot went from huge to astronomic.

Longarm casually spread his boot heels and bent his knees just a tad as he braced himself to draw as fast as he might need to. For the one called Fandango was bluffing like a puff adder against a slick dealer named for sky-limit stakes, and hadn't One-Eyed Jack run the pot way up in the sky more than once before winning the sure way, with a gun?

By now it had narrowed down to just Sky Kirby and Fandango, if that wasn't really One-Eyed Jack in the flesh. Longarm had to keep his eyes on all the others in the crowded room as he braced for Lord only knew what. For surely a cuss aiming to take the pot with a gun didn't expect to back out through the door with all that . . . Hold on, there was nothing on that fool table but *chips*! So how could One-Eyed Jack and any number of confederates hope to shoot their way out and still cash in?

"Somebody's gone *loco en la cabeza*," Longarm told himself as Fandango raised again. It wasn't going to work. A poker bluff would only carry a player as high as his own line of credit went, and Sky Kirby could see any bet by any player less well heeled than, say, Saratoga Canfield or Bet-A-Million Gates.

Then Sky Kirby proved conventional card wisdom wrong by folding with a wry little smile and saying, "I don't suppose you'd care to show me what you were really holding, Fandango?"

Fandango purred, "It'll cost you another thousand." Then, as Sky Kirby murmured something wistful about barely breaking even on that silver claim, the man who'd beaten him by a brass-balled bluff raked in the pot and said, "I hate to be a spoilsport. But my dear old momma told me to quit while I was ahead if I ever got ahead. So where do I cash these chips in, gents?"

Sky Kirby reached under his frock coat as he said, "The bank, which is me, naturally writes you a check, Fandango. Neither you nor anyone else with a lick of sense wants to pack that much cash around with the local law just about extinct."

He spread the checkbook on the table and uncapped a fancy gold fountain pen as he continued. "This check's drawn on a Denver bank, but you'll find you can cash it here or Leadville."

Longarm had heard all he cared to. None of it made much sense to him, but he couldn't see either Kirby or the younger cuss who'd played him for a sucker as One-Eyed Jack, unless One-Eyed Jack had worked out a new, less violent way to leave town with a pot he hadn't won fair and square.

He'd told Poker Alice he'd get back to her. She might see an angle he had to be missing as well. But as he strode back along the walk in the gathering dusk, that black coffee he'd inhaled to stay awake worked its way through his kidneys. So he ducked into a narrow slot between two shuttered shops to take a discreet leak.

He was just buttoning up again when he heard clunking boot heels and some asshole saying, "I'm sure he headed this way, and I meant what I said about cleaning his plow!"

Longarm wasn't sure who they were talking about until another voice said soothingly, "We was there when he complained about your singing, Windy. But Fandango told you to let it be, and he'd likely clean *your* plow entire if you draw attention to us just as he's set to ride out with better than thirty grand in honest winnings!"

Longarm drew his six-gun and held his breath as they argued some more about him within spitting distance. Then their boot heels were clunking back the way they'd come, and Longarm put his .44-40 away, muttering, "What in blue blazes am I *missing* here?"

He knew he was missing something. He realized now that Fandango and his pals had been the rowdies he'd stopped from scattering Edwina's herd. Even if Fandango himself was a tad more sensible than the total assholes he rode with,

he'd still bluffed ten years' salary for a top hand out of . . .
a high-rolling gambler who'd been dealing from the bottom
and had doubtless known what he was holding?

"I better talk to Poker Alice," Longarm muttered aloud as
he strode on. "I'm sure as hell missing something here about
poker!"

Chapter 13

The back room of the Hornsilver Saloon was smaller, but so were the game and the table stakes of silver dollars. Poker Alice asked an even older but more neatly put-together geezer to take over while she had a private motherly talk with her nephew Ginger.

They went out front and bellied up to the bar like men as Poker Alice murmured, "The one inside with the chin whiskers and pug hat would be Trevor Crockett. I asked how often he got over the pass to Leadville, and I don't think he's the one you want, Custis. He told me, and got no argument from other miners inside, he hadn't been out of this valley since they put him to work in the Blue Devil shaft."

Longarm signaled the barkeep they'd both have needled beer, and said he hoped she'd questioned Crockett sort of discreetly.

Poker Alice stated demurely, "I'm always discreet, be it male, female, or my own fingers I'm in love with at the time. I naturally never said I was acting in the name of the law. I said I had me some money to wire home and asked if he'd be headed for Leadville again in the near future. When he asked me where I'd got the notion he'd be headed there at all, I repeated your suggestion about dynamite caps and said,

120

real casual, I'd heard he'd posted some letters for others here in Holy Cross."

As they got their needled beers she added, "Thanks. Crockett allowed I had him mixed up with somebody else. He said the owners of the shaft he works in buy the dynamite and such he works with. I didn't even have to pry deeper. Big Jim Fagan, the one with the spade beard inside, volunteered he sells the mining supplies in question. He says he has 'em packed over the Divide by mule train, and that explains why he's so cheerful when he loses. He has to be making a heap, selling everything you need to dig silver, whether you wind up with any silver or not!"

Longarm said he recalled the merchant, and they both inhaled some suds. Poker Alice offered suggestions about others in town who rode back and forth on occasion. The trouble was, she failed to tie any in to that back-shot barkeep who'd been fixing to turn One-Eyed Jack in.

He told her about the other game he'd just witnessed. She grimaced and said, "That Sky Kirby bets too steep and crazy for my blood. I can see why he's using chips instead of cash for table stakes, though. A twenty-grand pot in spend-able form would tempt the angels, or even me, to just throw down on the house and grab it. You know by now how many card-table fights over so-called dirty dealings are just excuses for plain old-fashioned holdups!"

It hadn't been a question. Longarm still answered, "I do. I was half expecting Fandango to pull a stunt like that when I saw how he was bluffing. But he couldn't. Then Sky Kirby wrote him out a check for the full amount and . . . Hold on. Might not a man meaning to bet pure wind and pay off with bad checks have a good reason to fib about selling a mining claim for a hundred grand, whether he'd sold it or not? Everyone I've asked seems to feel Miss Clara Drakmanton's good for the money."

Poker Alice sipped more suds. "She is, if she's that same Clara Drakmanton who builds houses and holds shares in that streetcar company with Hod Tabor. She's all right. I knew her daddy before her, down to Pikes Peak just before the war. He left her well off to begin with, and she's run the family placer claim into a real fortune."

Longarm frowned thoughtfully. "That's odd. I got the notion, talking to her, she didn't know that much about mining."

Poker Alice shrugged. "Doubt she would know much about hardrocking silver. Like I said, her daddy panned for gold, and they say he sent her to some business school. She ain't mixed up in mining over in Pueblo or Leadville. Anyone growing up near mining knows how a mining man has to pay for everything from his boot heels up, whether digging diamonds or rabbit turds."

She finished her schooner and signaled for two more. "My turn. I can afford that luxury at least. Sometimes I wish I'd had the sense to take one of the bigger pots I've won in my time and go into some less risky business, such as a notions shop or boardinghouse. Hod Tabor switched from cards to groceries less than ten years back, and look at him now. Maybe next time, if I ever win enough to buy me some business property . . . But I dunno. Real estate's selling for two hundred fifty dollars a front foot in Leadville right now, and it costs as much five hundred dollars a month to rent a store along Chestnut or Harrison. That's before you stock it, and they say you can rent stores in New York City for less!"

Longarm said he could see how Clara Drakmanton had been able to refuse the unproven Silver Spoon claim, and added, "She'll likely survive Kirby's welshing on their loco bet as well."

Poker Alice said, "Sky Kirby may be loco. He bets sky high on some mighty odd things at ridiculous odds. But he don't welsh. No professional does, if they value their reps.

I've been down to where I had go without supper and sleep out under the stars, Custis. But I've yet to fail to honor my markers."

She swallowed some beer, grimaced, and continued. "A sporting gal or card-playing gent depends on others trusting 'em to make good on their word sooner or later. For sometimes your word is all you have to bet as you wait for your luck to change. I don't like Sky Kirby. I think he's a blowhard and I've long suspected he cheats. But if he offered me his marker I'd take it. For say what you may about the old basser, he always pays off when he loses."

Longarm muttered, "He sure lost a lot tonight. Twenty grand to a bluffer would hurt even if he'd really sold that hundred-grand claim. I don't see how any gambler could roll so high, wide, and foolish and still keep paying off."

Poker Alice suggested, "Even a fool has to *win* now and again. I figure he uses his sky-high rep and almost unlimited credit to just bully his way to the pot a lot. Nobody holding less than a mighty rare royal flush can be sure he knows what he's doing as the stakes go up and up and then up some more. From what you say about his game with this Fandango, Sky could have been holding anything or nothing."

Longarm finished his second schooner and covered the empty with his hand as he grumbled, "Sky was dealing, and unless my eyesight's failing, he was dealing exactly what he wanted everyone to have!"

Poker Alice asked, "Are you saying he lost to Fandango on purpose?"

Before Longarm could answer she pointed out, "Let's assume that Fandango was his long-lost bastard child and a doting daddy was out to pay for his education. Then let's ask ourselves why a dirty dealer dealt him a worthless hand instead of, say, all aces and faces?"

Longarm sighed. "Remind me never to play poker with you, Miss Alice. I don't seem to know the game as well as

I thought. For I must have been wrong about one of those rascals or the other. Sky Kirby must have just been dealing clumsy instead of sneaky. Is that considered natural in your fraternity, Miss Alice?"

She shook her head. "Not when you give a damn about the game. You're right. We're both missing something. But meantime, I got to get back to my own game. You coming, Custis?"

He decided he'd hardly get any more out of the boys in the back room than he'd already gotten from Poker Alice. So they shook on it and parted friendly.

He thought about drifting back to that other game. But then he thought about those sore losers looking for him, and decided he'd as soon not risk a fight just to prove what everyone agreed upon when it came to Sky Kirby. The high roller bet like a greenhorn, paid off when he lost sucker bets, and still had the money to tear-ass all over in a coach and four with a corporal's squad of bodyguards.

He remembered he'd told Clara Drakmanton he'd get back to her, and since it was getting later by the minute as he chased himself around in circles, he headed back to his hotel.

The moon was high above the valley, and an old gent had just lit a street lamp in front of the hotel. Longarm idly noted the lettering on that false front next door as he crossed over, thinking back to that rifleman up behind it. He still had no idea whether the kid from Coal Creek had been after him or poor old Blackfoot Blake. The mean little shit had fired through that gap in the boards above the letter *R* of . . . FAGAN'S HARDWARE?

Longarm almost turned around to go back and ask more questions as he recalled what Poker Alice had said about the bearded Big Jim Fagan selling dynamite caps and doubtless rifle rounds. But then he realized he'd bought his own ammo, socks, and soap long before arriving and decided he wasn't ready to flash his badge yet.

There was no way to ask a store owner the rude sort of questions he had in mind without flashing a badge at him. And there were more subtle ways to find out whether a local businessman had been over the pass about the time Billy Vail had gotten that wire from the late Sean O'Hanlon.

Longarm went on inside the hotel. There was nobody at all on duty behind the desk now. They were likely filled up, and like himself, everyone with a lick of sense in a small hotel kept their room keys on hand as they came and went.

He went on up, saw light under the door of Clara Drakmanton's room next to his own, and knocked. She asked who it was before she opened her door. Once she did, he saw she looked mighty worried. She wore the same kimono, but had let down and dry-brushed her long auburn hair. She said, "Ginger! I was about to come looking for you. I heard funny noises downstairs before. But when I went down there was nobody there and . . . where have you been all this time?"

He smiled thinly. "I'm afraid you missed the chance to ride back to Leadville with the Chaffee outfit. I'm still working on who might or might not go back and forth fairly often. After that I dropped in on a couple of card games, and you'll never guess what Sky Kirby told us all about you. He seems to think you've already left town, by the way."

She shut the door behind him and shot the bolt as he went on to tell her how Sky Kirby had said she'd bought that mining claim after all. She waved him to a seat on the edge of her bed and sat down beside him as she marveled, "Why on earth would he want to lie about me like that?"

Longarm took off his hat and unbuttoned his jacket all the way, since she'd shut the sash against the evening breezes and burned a lot of coal oil up there waiting for him all that time.

He said, "Another high roller I consulted didn't think he wanted to lie about you, Miss Clara. He wanted to lie about himself, or how much ready cash he had on hand."

When she repeated she hadn't given Sky Kirby a dime, he hushed her with a finger to his own lips and explained, "I'm sure old Sky noticed. His brag about selling his silver claim was likely meant to assure everyone he had at least a hundred grand to bet with as he raised the ante ever higher and . . . Hold on. That ain't what he done. He folded, to a pure bluff, when the pot was twenty grand and not all of it his money."

She said she didn't know that much about cards. He chuckled and admitted, "I seem to have a lot to learn as well. But all right, I still say he lied about you giving him all that money for a silver claim everyone knew he'd won earlier because he wants everyone to think he . . . don't own it no more."

She said she didn't know what he was talking about. He said that made two of them, adding, "Bet-A-Million Gates stretches the truth about winning and losing fortunes making loco bets. But in point of fact he's really a big-time bob-wire salesman who improves his sales by being famous. Bob wire is bob wire, so all things being close to equal, lots of stockmen would as soon buy a hundred miles of wire off somebody famous as a nobody they never heard of."

She asked what selling fencing had to do with Sky Kirby. He said, "Nothing. He's supposed to be a gambler pure and simple. It hurts a gambler to be known as a cheat or a welsher. It might help a tad with some players to be known as a good loser who can lose. But it ain't as if Saratoga Canfield would have twenty grand to blow on advertising, and there's that one thousand Kirby just handed you on a silver platter, as if money didn't mean a thing to him!"

The sharp young businesswoman who'd gone to school to learn what money was suggested, "Maybe it doesn't. What if he owns a secret gold mine, or a counterfeiting press?"

Longarm smiled thinly and said, "Already considered both. A man with private unlimited funds would have no call to be a professional gambler, and that's what Sky Kirby seems to be. He surely doesn't work at anything else, and seems to have no use for investments as solid as a silver claim."

She repeated her other suggestion.

He shook his head and said, "There ain't been that much queer, or counterfeit, floating around out our way. He paid that Fandango off with a twenty-grand check drawn on a big Denver bank. There's that one thousand in cash for you, sitting in the safe of a first-class hotel in Leadville. How would you deposit twenty-five or more thousand dollars in queer with any hope of getting away with it? Queer-passers break a bill and run with the change before the first professional bank teller spots it."

She shrugged, moving the mattress under them a shade, and said she'd always wondered how they'd detect a perfect counterfeit if anyone ever made a perfect counterfeit.

He shook his head and said, "Government mints have tried, and it still won't work for long. Paper money has to be backed by bullion. Prices would start rising and just keep going up if ever they tried fake gold and silver coinage or printed money backed by no more than a politician's promise. So faking coins with some tricky alloy would cost too much to make any profit, whilst paper money has to have a heap of different serial numbers so's the treasury can record the demands for bullion whenever spoilsports ask for the real thing."

She brightened and said, "Oh, that's right. It does say the U.S. Treasury will pay the bearer bullion on demand. So a man depositing even twenty thousand in worthless paper in a Denver bank would be taking a dreadful chance, wouldn't he?"

Longarm said, "He would indeed. The Denver Mint's near Colfax and Broadway, and a heap of old-timers withdraw from their own bank deposits in silver and gold. So a Denver bank would be likely to try to cash your deposited queer most any time. Wouldn't matter how good your paper and

127

printing was. They'd trip you up at the mint with those serial numbers."

Clara Drakmanton nodded soberly and said, "So he's neither the Count of Monte Cristo nor a counterfeiter. Would you mind telling me what you are, Ginger?"

Longarm was still making up his mind how to answer the unexpected question when she insisted, "You would have ridden back with that cattle outfit if you'd really been riding with them. You haven't been looking for work in this mining town, and yet you've the money for as fine a room as this next door."

He said, "I only paid six bits."

But she said, "You have to be riding for the law, if you're not riding well outside it. So can you blame a girl for feeling just a little nervous about you?"

He sighed and rose to his feet, saying, "Nope. I'd make me as nervous if I was a maiden pure. I ain't ready to lay all my cards on the table, Miss Clara. If I told you why, that would be a card in its own right. So I'll just say *buenoches* and let you get some beauty rest."

But as he took his hat off the bedpost she sprang up to slide between him and the door, pleading, "For heaven's sake, you can't just leave me hanging in suspense! Never mind how pure I am, and tell me who you are and what's really going on!"

He smiled down at her and said, "I don't know what's going on. If I did, I'd know better who I could trust with my own little secrets. If it's any comfort, I've no call to crook you or arrest you, as far as I know, no matter who I might be."

He tried to sidle around her. He hadn't noticed how firm her considerable curves were until then. As she barred his exit with her shapely body against his, she almost wept. "You don't trust me! You think I'm some sort of crook too, and all sorts of folks in these mountains will vouch for me, Ginger!"

He almost told her Poker Alice already had. He didn't because other weepy ladies in the past had taught him how much a fool man can give away in what seems harmless conversation with them. He said, "I trust you as much as I trust anyone else around here, and you're taking unfair advantage of me, Miss Clara. It's getting late, and this is rapidly progressing beyond belly-to-belly into cruelty to animals!"

He knew she knew exactly what she was doing as she thrust her kimono-clad pelvis against his denim-covered right thigh, clear of his six-gun, and insisted, "You're the one who's being cruel. It's not so late, and how do you expect a girl to get a wink of sleep as she wonders about you in the very next room down the hall?"

He said, "There ain't that much to wonder about me, now that I see you've got my full attention against your inner thigh, and I'm sure you've noticed!"

She coyly replied, "I was wondering if you had another gun or really liked me."

So he laughed, tossed his hat aside, and took her in both arms to plant a friendly kiss on her pretty upturned face as she got to grinding downright shamelessly against his jeans.

He wondered why they were wasting all that effort with so many duds in the way. So he swept her up off her slippered feet, moved back to the bed, and flopped them both down to unfasten her sash and run his free hand down her smooth bare belly as they kissed a tad more friendly. She stiffened as she felt his questing fingers parting her auburn hair down yonder, and hissed, "For heaven's sake, trim the lamp!"

So he rolled off her to do so, plunging the room into almost total darkness, save for the wan glow of the street lamp outside through the lace curtains. He hung his gun over one bedpost and his hat on another, but let his boots and duds land anywhere they might want to in his hurry to rejoin her on the bed.

When he did, he found she'd shucked her kimono too, and slid a pillow under her hips without being asked. So he knew she was a modern woman to make Miss Victoria Woodhull proud, and figured she was just complimenting him when she gasped, "Oh, my God, what are you trying to shove inside me, Ginger?"

Then he did, but felt he ought to ask politely if she needed some time to get used to it. She moved her own hips up his shaft as she sobbed, "It feels lovely, Ginger. I want you to ravage me to the depths of my being with that marvel of nature, and I want you to come in me and come again and again!"

He was willing to try. Most men would have been. For even in the dark she felt mighty handsome and smelled divine. But thanks to his earlier ravaging right next door, he didn't come as soon as most men might have in anything that swell. But the passionate young redhead didn't seem at all insulted. She gasped, "Yes! Yes! Keep going just that way and don't ever stop, Ginger!"

He was starting to feel it was safe to tell her his friends all called him Custis in bed. But that was why some sneaky women were inclined to go to bed with secretive gents. They said that really patriotic Miss Belle Siddons had damn near won the war for the South by screwing military secrets out of Union staff officers. A man was likely to say anything when he was coming in a beautiful woman. But as he finally shot his wad in the beautiful Clara, he was proud to say nothing more revealing than that he'd never had as great a lay and meant to stay right there with her forever and ever. He knew half the nice things she said to him as she came twice to his harder effort would never stand up in the court of a cold gray dawn. Lovers were a lot like drunks getting bailed out ahead of others they'd spent a night in the tank with. They meant all they said at the time they were saying it. No gal smart enough to run her own business, read Victoria Woodhull, and likely

130

pine for the right to vote should expect any man to leave it soaking in her forever and a day. So he finally took it out, and sure enough, she smoked between times too. He was glad she didn't tell him, as they shared one of his cheroots, who'd taught her such swell bad habits. It took a really experienced lover to just make love, with no justifying tales of earlier woe. So how come he was so curious about whether she'd been broken in as a mining-town tomboy or back at that fancy business school? He laughed and said, "You know, that could be the answer to Sky Kirby. Mystery is so interesting that some folks act mysterious just to seem interesting. If they'd ever found Captain Kidd's treasure, it would have likely added up to a few dollars' worth of knickknacks, and the mystery of the *Mary Celeste* would have gone down as just another square-rigger lost at sea if she hadn't been found afloat and abandoned so mysteriously."

Clara took a languorous drag on the cheroot they were sharing and asked why he was being so mysterious.

He laughed and said, "I ain't just showing off. But what if Sky Kirby just enjoys confounding folks by doing something loco now and again? A cheater at cards might aim to give the impression he dealt honest by losing now and again on purpose. He'd have to lose big for word to get around. But it can't hurt that much to lose any amount of money you never worked for, and who's to say he really loses all of it? Everyone there tonight saw him write out that handsome check for Fandango, another mysterious cuss. But who's to say, or even wonder, whether Fandango ever cashes that check or not? You wouldn't even need a real bank account if you only wrote out checks to your shills, see?"

She stiffened in the darkness beside him and snapped, "Why, you suspicious brute! Are you saying I was only going along with some scheme to make Sky Kirby look reckless with his money?"

He reached across her to snub out the smoke, her bare nipples pressed to his bare chest, as he said, "Five hundred in a hotel safe is way less than twenty grand on a paper check, honey. I just said it was easy money and he was using a known rich lady to make some of us think he'd just sold a silver claim for a hundred grand. I know you weren't in cahoots with him, you pretty little thing."

As he ran a friendly hand over her naked torso, she asked what made him so certain, seeing he didn't trust her enough to tell her his real name.

He kissed her, rolled her on her well-padded chest, and rose to mount her from behind as he explained conversationally, "Had the two of you been working together to make it look as if he'd just sold a silver claim, the two of you wouldn't have gone through such a rain dance. Instead of betting on whether you'd buy or not, you'd have just written him a big check to flash, and caused even more of a show by signing deeds and such in front of the justice of the peace down the street."

He swung one foot to the rug and lifted her hipbones with his palms to fit them together better dog-style as he said, "He made that sucker bet with you to get you to ride over here and show your well-known self to any skeptics. He never expected a miner's daughter to buy an unproven claim for a hundred grand after Hook and Rische sold a one-third share in their Little Pittsburgh to a grocer named Tabor for less than a hundred dollars' worth of supplies and corn liquor."

She arched her back and thrust her rump higher to meet his thrusts as he planted both feet on the rug to really throw it to her, inspired by the new angle and the teasing blur of bare buttocks in the dim light from outside. She moaned that she was glad he didn't think she was a bad girl, and begged him to ram it to her harder. So the bed springs were creaking pretty good when, out in the hall, it got much noisier!

"Kee-rist!" cried Longarm as he grabbed for his own gun on the bedpost, even as he hauled out of the equally startled Clara. He ran naked as a jay, gun in hand, across the rug and out in to the dark hallway just as somebody else was crawfishing out the door of Longarm's empty room in a thick cloud of gunsmoke, a sawed-off double Greener in hand!

Longarm threw down on the dark outline, yelling, "Drop that gun and grab some sky!"

But while the intruder let go of the shotgun he'd emptied into Longarm's empty bed, he still went for the six-gun on his right hip. So Longarm fired, and the tough rascal still kept trying to draw as he reeled back down the hall, getting hit thrice more on his feet and once in his back for luck before Longarm clicked his own gun's hammer on an empty chamber and ran forward, feeling as dumb as any other stark-naked man in a hotel hallway as he dropped to one bare knee, felt the side of the downed assassin's throat, and muttered, "Don't go away. I got to put some pants on!"

He ran back inside just as other doors began to open cautiously. As somebody yelled, "My God, there's a dead man out here!" Longarm shut and bolted the door of Clara's room, saying, "He's right. You better get dressed too, honey. I suspicion this place is going to get crowded as hell before long."

She rolled upright to grab for her kimono as she gasped, "Oh, Lord, they told me across the way that all the lawmen in town are out searching for those other outlaws!"

He said, "They are. I reckon that makes me it. You were bound to find out sooner or later, honey. So I'd be U.S. Deputy Custis Long."

She laughed like hell and said, "Pleased to meet you, Longarm, and it's nice to know whose cum I feel running down my thigh at the moment, you horny thing!"

Chapter 14

By the time Lawford's Last Post got really crowded, Longarm had his federal badge pinned to the front of his hickory shirt and his reloaded .44-40 was riding sedately on his denim-clad hip. It hadn't taken long, so he was still mighty confused himself by the spade-bearded body on the hallway floor, still oozing on the bare planking in the light of the hall sconce Longarm had relit.

He wondered how many others were fixing to say it when yet a fourth townsman crowding around gasped, "Jesus H. Christ! It's Big Jim Fagan from the right next door!"

A somewhat older townsman who'd been there when Blackfoot Blake was shot opined, "That explains how that kid from Coal Creek got up on that roof with that Creedmoor! Big Jim must have let him up on his roof from inside on the sly."

Longarm was too modest to say who the real target might have been. But then that young Indian maid came out of the room he'd hired next to Clara's to announce, "Somebody shot all the stuffings out of your mattress, Mister Ginger!"

Longarm nodded down at her and replied, "I noticed. Where have you been all this time, miss?"

The gal pointed at the body at their feet. "Mister Fagan sent me on an errand. He gave me a note to take to Mrs. Lawford up the valley. But when I finally got there they told me she'd never gone there to begin with. So I rested up a little and started back. I was only a few furlongs off when I heard all that shooting. Why do you suppose Mister Fagan did that?"

Longarm said, "Good help is hard to find. Reckon he decided to do it himself after his hired hand from Coal Creek fared so poor. How come you felt obliged to take orders from a shopkeeper next door, seeing you work here, Miss . . . ?"

"Owlfeather, Columbine Owlfeather," she replied, going on to explain. "Mister Fagan owns this hotel too. Didn't you know that?"

Longarm whistled softly. "I do now. Widow Lawford told me she did, albeit come to study on it, an army widow doesn't get get all that much off the War Department. I'll take your word this sneaky cuss was some sort of silent partner, Miss Columbine. Where do you reckon the widow really wound up this evening if it wasn't where . . . Hold on, did *she* tell you she was visiting up the valley, or was it Fagan here?"

The Indian girl said Fagan had. So Longarm asked the pretty little gal to go see if she could find her lavender-haired boss.

He was going through Fagan's pockets when Clara came out in the hall in that shantung riding outfit, looking as if butter wouldn't melt in her mouth. She said she'd never seen the dead rascal. Longarm told her and everyone else in the crowded hallway, "He's got all kinds of papers proving him all sorts of names from all sort of other places, along with this Lake County voter's registration made out to James H. Fagan. Riders along the owlhoot trail like to take out a library card here and register to vote there under names their elders never gave 'em."

135

He held up a library card to the light, whistled softly, and added, "Now this is surely interesting. Whether he was sporting this same beard or not at the time, he was borrowing books close enough to a certain Indian agency to suggest a good motive for a shotgun call on a federal deputy!"

He rose to his considerable full height, putting the varied pieces of identification in his own shirt pocket for the time being as he grumbled, "I sure wish you all had a Western Union here in Holy Cross. I got a heap of wheels within wheels going here, and no way to be sure without wiring a few questions hither and yon in the outside world."

They all heard the same piercing scream from downstairs. Longarm was still the one who got there first as young Columbine Owlfeather came out a dark doorway, sobbing, "He killed her! He cut her throat and bled her like an old hog!"

Longarm stepped around the distraught gal and struck a Mex waterproof match made of wax as he entered what seemed to be the widow woman's private quarters. She lay face up across her bed, her kimono flung wide to expose her well-formed naked corpse as her lavender-haired head hung over the side towards the doorway, her dead face smiling blankly up at them upside down. Columbine had been right about her bleeding from that gashed-open throat. There was still-sticky blood a quarter inch deep as far as the doorsill. Columbine sobbed, "He left her like that, naked. Do you suppose . . . before he cut her throat he . . . you know?"

It would have sounded crude to suggest the killer had gone sloppy seconds. It felt spooky to consider his own sperm might still be alive inside that cooling corpse. From the way she was starting to grin, mirthless as hell, he figured she'd been dead from three to six hours. He counted silently in his head and muttered, mostly to himself, "Not long after she came down from up yonder, pretending to be mortified when, in truth, she'd found out all she could for One-Eyed Jack and wanted to report to him in full."

Columbine asked, "Who's One-Eyed Jack?"

But he didn't have to go into it because by then most of the others, including Clara, had crowded round. He'd already figured Clara was a nice gal, but he liked her even better when she struck a light of her own, gasped, and said, "Oh, the poor thing, we have to cover her with a sheet at least!"

As she started to step inside, Longarm said, "Hold it. The floor is awash in half-dried blood!"

But Clara just hoisted her skirts a mite with one hand and declared, "My riding boots are dubbed with beeswax as well as calf-high, and I'd hate to have anyone see *me* in that position!"

As she gingerly stepped into the death chamber, young Columbine gulped and murmured, "She was always nice to me." Then she followed Clara.

A local man in bib overalls volunteered, "The dead rascal has a whole barrel of sweeping sawdust next door, Marshal, if we have your permission to bust in."

Longarm shook his head and said, "I'm a deputy marshal and you don't. I want to keep as much as possible under lock and key till I can take inventory with somebody from Fagan's bank."

A better-dressed man in the lower hallway said, "That would be me, and I'm curious as hell too! Big Jim Fagan built this hotel and the shop next door paying cash on the barrel head. But he naturally started a savings and checking account with us as soon as we put up our own business. I'd be A. M. Cooper of Prospector's Trust. We're a branch of the main office you may have heard of in Leadville."

Longarm allowed he'd been by their Leadville headquarters, and told the other local in overalls to come along and get some of that sawdust.

Poker Alice, Trevor Crockett, and some of the others who'd been playing cards with Fagan earlier were waiting out on the walk. When Poker Alice spied the badge worn openly on

Longarm's breast she almost sobbed, "It was all my fault. We just now heard he tried to gun you like he gunned Blackfoot Blake. He tricked me back at the saloon by saying he knew you from Leadville and was wondering about your reasons for pretending to be somebody else, Custis."

Longarm said soothingly, "Lord only knows what *I* might have given away whilst . . . conversing with his secret partner, Miss Alice. I ain't so sure they were behind the killing of Marshal Blake, though. A man would be a fool to aim at lawmen from his own property, and the hotel next door works better. It's way easier to lie in wait behind a lace curtain than atop a roof, exposed to the Lord and anyone inclined to crane their necks at a rifle shot."

As they tagged after him next door he suggested, "Try her this way. Say that kid with the Creedmoor slithered up the slit betwixt this hardware and the hotel next door on his own. Nobody inside or out front noticed. The hotel wall overlooking the gently sloping roof is blank. So he just skulked behind the false front till his target came out of the marshal's office across the way, just as his killer had every right to expect."

The door to the hardware was naturally locked. That didn't mean much to a lawman packing a pocketknife with an unlawfully worked blade. As he was picking the lock the banker said, "If young Penn wasn't working for Fagan or the widow next door, he must have been working for somebody else! He had no call to gun our marshal on his own!"

Longarm said, "He might have been after *me*. But you're likely right about the owners of this here property. If Fagan was really the outlaw I was sent here after, neither he nor his female partner had any call to be expecting me in particular. I drifted into town incognito, and they'd have only noticed me after I'd arrived mighty noisy out front. I don't want to give a lecture on it, but if Fagan was really my man, he must have been mighty chagrined when other outlaws commenced to roll off his roof and I seemed to take some interest in his immediate surroundings."

He popped the latch and stepped inside. As he struck a light and lit a lamp by the doorway, they crowded in after him, with old Poker Alice in the lead.

As he swept his eyes over the cluttered shelves, noting there was no ladder leading up to the exposed beams of the sloping roof, Poker Alice said, "I can see why Big Jim was out to gun you if he was on your wanted list and feared you were getting warm, Custis. But why would he want to be so mean to Widow Lawford next door?"

Longarm moved over to the counter, saw the till was locked as well, and got to work on that as he explained. "She knew too much and he wasn't sure how well she was getting to know me. If he was really who I'm pretty sure he was, she was the one poor Sean O'Hanlon entrusted with the fatal secret that Big Jim Fagan might also be One-Eyed Jack McBride!"

When someone said the late O'Hanlon had stayed at the hotel next door when he wasn't tending bar, the banker, Cooper, volunteered, "We were told Fagan had sold her the hotel for a dollar and other considerations. What do you reckon those other considerations might have been?"

Longarm silenced the round of dirty snickers and told them not to speak ill of the dead, adding, "Had she been as dedicated to evil as him, he might not have felt he had to kill her. I happen to know she seemed sort of sweet and friendly. She can't confirm this now, but I suspect her hotel guest recognized the shopkeeper next door as the notorious One-Eyed Jack and confided in her, offering to share the considerable reward with her if only she'd send a wire for him the next time she got over to Leadville on business. It's possible he even asked her to make it her business to go shopping for hotel soap and such in Leadville. He didn't know she could get all the hotel supplies she wanted from the real owner of her hotel.

O'Hanlon was naturally tied down by his twelve-hour-a-day job at the saloon."

He popped the lock of the till as he continued. "Like I said, she wasn't such a mean old gal. She likely told her secret partner O'Hanlon was on to him out of simple loyalty. There'd have been no reason for him to tell her he meant to silence O'Hanlon for good after she or mayhaps he himself sent the fool wire. Once O'Hanlon was dead, she'd have felt she was in too deep to back out. So she played his game while your town law and some deputies from my Denver office asked all the wrong questions in all the wrong places."

There was naturally nothing but small change in the till after business hours. But he found a neatly folded sheet of newsprint to spread open on the countertop as he went on. "I'd like to think a nicer sneak was against killing me as well once Fagan or One-Eyed Jack began to suspect me. They might have argued about that, or some more personal matter. At any rate, he got rid of the hired help and killed her silently before trying to kill me less subtly with a ten-gauge Greener. Lord knows how he meant to explain both our bodies. Mayhaps he felt he might not have to. Nobody bothered him about the killing of Sean O'Hanlon, right?"

By this time he'd scanned the single front page of a back-dated newspaper from way out of town. He whistled softly and explained to the others, "I don't know why so many of 'em return to the scenes of their crimes neither. This one was trying to be slicker. But I once caught a road agent kind enough to be packing his own wanted poster, complete with his description, in his saddlebag. One-Eyed Jack must have sent for this paper well after he'd ridden off with enough Indian Agency money for a fresh start and a new life here."

The banker craned to read the headlines, and pointed out that nothing at all about the missing funds was mentioned on the page. So Longarm pointed at the masthead and said, "Scene of the crime. The fairly distant township on the far side of the Divide where a worried killer *did* help himself to enough money for a new start in the hardware and hotel business. It must have made him feel smarter when he sent away for the paper and found things had commenced to cool off. He may have saved this one page because of the article on the same sheriff running for re-election this fall. But I ain't so worried about why he did it. Like I said, a heap of 'em *do*. It must be something like probing a bad tooth with your tongue. Common sense says not to do it. But you do it anyway."

The banker agreed Big Jim had been dumb to go after a lawman with Longarm's rep in the dark, and opined there'd be enough in the bank accounts of the two cadavers to bury them both in style as soon as the justice of the peace down the way probated their considerable estates.

Longarm shook his head and warned, "I'd hold that grand notion and store both bodies somewhere cool till I can get word to my home office and the Bureau of Indian Affairs. Uncle Sam is going to want to go over their books before he releases a dime less than One-Eyed Jack stole from him. As Big Jim Fagan, he may or may not have made some profits at his new career as a boom-town businessman. Meanwhile, I'd best impound everything and lock up till Uncle Sam can hold a real inventory here!"

As he locked the small change away and herded everyone toward the front, Poker Alice said, "Hold on. Ain't you forgetting something, Custis? If that kid on the roof from Coal Creek wasn't working for One-Eyed Jack and Widow Lawford, who in thunder *was* he working for?"

Longarm suggested, "Let's eat the apple a bite at a time, Miss Alice. Either posse might come back with some answers to that one."

She said, "What if they don't?"

To which he could only reply, "Somebody else will have to find out. I ain't even sure I've solved the riddle of One-Eyed Jack yet!"

He blew out the lamp by the door, and commenced to lock up with a padlock from the store's own stock as he continued. "Got nothing but a heap of guesses that add up sort of neat so far. Got to make sure of at least half my guesses before it's safe to say we can close the books on anybody."

The banker said he was already convinced, adding, "I feel sort of dumb about it now. But do you know Widow Lawford never cashed one government check here in town, even though she told us all she was on an army pension!"

Longarm nodded soberly. "Reckon she didn't want to say where she had got the money to open a hotel here in Holy Cross. The nameless soldier blue she told me she was still pining for would be tough to track down at this late date. But there ain't all that many married officers on your average army post, and she did say she and her husband had spent time at Fort Benton and Fort Hood. Someone at one or the other would surely recall whether they'd ever quartered a couple named Lawford or not."

Poker Alice said, "Who are you going to ask about that kid on the roof with that Creedmoor?"

He repeated what he'd said about eating apples, and suggested they all get a good night's sleep and an early start on asking questions in the morning.

Nobody argued. He was the law.

It wasn't any clearer inside who Longarm and Clara Drakmanton owed for another night's rent. But once all the bodies had been hauled off and things had simmered down again, a good time was had by all, and they even got some sleep before sunrise.

It wasn't easy. Old Clara seemed to feel he owed her a honeymoon worth of climaxes in one night, seeing he wouldn't be riding back over the pass with her no matter how she pleaded.

Once the worn-out if not fully satisfied Clara fell asleep, he relit their lamp and composed a dozen messages he wanted Western Union to put on the wire over in Leadville.

When he handed her the pages torn from his notebook over their breakfast across the street the next morning, Clara said she'd be proud to send them for him and relay any answers back by way of trustworthy riders on the heavily traveled trail. All she asked in return was his promise he'd stop by her place in Pueblo on his way back to Denver.

He gave her his word. He knew he'd likely be up to kissing a face that pretty some more, once he rested up a spell.

He asked her to get word to him when and if she picked up her winnings on that loco bet with Sky Kirby. She said she would, but asked, "Surely you don't think he was in league with One-Eyed Jack and that poor old widow woman, do you?"

He gazed wistfully down at his flapjacks as unbidden but mighty nice memories of a gray-haired twat taking it dog-style got in the way of his answer. "I don't know what Sky Kirby may or may not be up to. Up near the pass he as much as told me he was gunning for me. But more recently he tried to use me to verify his version of his deal with you. Let's just say I'd like to know whether he meant to pay off on that sucker bet or not."

She said she hoped so, after all that riding high and low with the fool gambler. Then she reached across the table to pat the back of his hand, purring, "Last night was worth it, even if he welshes on our bet. But aren't we putting the cart before the horse, dear? I have to get back to Leadville before I can do anything, and you've refused to ride back with me, you mean thing!"

He repeated what he'd said about having to tidy up in Holy Cross before he rode anywhere, and suggested they might know at the livery if anyone at all respectable was headed back over the Divide in the near future.

She wanted to go with him. So he let her, and they did better than just ask the livery hands. Poker Alice was there, and she said she was leaving for certain if yet another gal wanted to ride along with her. She explained the pickings had been slimmer than she'd expected in Holy Cross and that the place was starting to spook her.

When Longarm asked just what she meant, Poker Alice said, "Can't put my finger on it, but there's something spooky going on, Custis. Such mining as there is seems mighty hardscrabble, with more being made trading in mineral futures than anyone's dug out of any rock. So there ain't that many paid-up mining men getting paid enough to play cards with the likes of me."

She relit her chewed-up cigar stub and continued. "At the same time, the few gents in town with real money seem to be high-rolling way over this child's head with the likes of Sky Kirby. I told you last night why I wouldn't play cards with him if I had that kind of money. So like I said, I'm headed back to Leadville where folks play poker sensibly!"

Clara Drakmanton told the hostler to saddle her mount while he was at it. Longarm said he'd fetch her saddlebags from the hotel. As he was leaving them for the moment he heard Poker Alice tell Clara, "I'd rather take my chances with Soapy Smith or that sickly Doc Holliday than the sinister characters I've met on this side of the pass. I mean, there's wild, and then there's downright snake-eyed, and I swear this town smells like a diamondback den in the greenup! Say, were you in Leadville that time Doc Holliday was selling them gold bricks?"

Longarm didn't hear the answer. He knew the story. Everybody did. Longarm wasn't sure he believed it. It sounded like the sort of flimflam Soapy Smith might pull, but Doc Holliday seemed a mite morose to charm suckers into buying fake gold bricks that had been supposed to be bars of bullion that had fallen off a dray. It made more sense if Soapy Smith had made the sales and the sinister Doc Holliday had played the part of the federal agent coming to confiscate the gold as government propery before it could be assayed.

Little Columbine Owlfeather was sitting in the lobby when he went inside. She asked him if he knew what she was supposed to do now that her boss lady lay on ice at the undertaker's. Longarm told her, "I understand the bank may ask for a lien on this hotel to make up for some outstanding business loans. They'd know better than me whether they mean to run the place themselves or sell it. In either case, they're likely to need some hired help. I can't tell you how long things may sort of drift in limbo. Meanwhile, how are you fixed for room and board, Miss Columbine?"

She sighed and said, "I've a garret room upstairs, and nobody's asked me to leave yet. But I don't know what I'll ever do for my eating money with Mrs. Lawford dead and owing me a month's back wages!"

Longarm whistled softly and reached in his jeans, saying he could let her have some pocket jingle till she got paid from the remains of the widow woman's estate once it was probated.

She gasped, "Oh, no, I couldn't take money from a strange man!"

He handed her a half eagle anyway, saying, "I ain't so strange and you ain't been listening, Miss Columbine. I never said I meant to *give* you anything. I'm only lending you enough to eat on till you can work something out with the new owners."

She stared down at the small gold coin in her dark palm and marveled, "You're trusting an Indian for ten whole dollars?"

He smiled innocently and asked, "What's your point? You told me you were a Kimoho Indian, didn't you?"

She nodded soberly and said, "Thank you. I mean to pay you back in full. I think I know who you must be now.

145

My people speak of a lawman they call Saltu Ka Saltu, the stranger who is no stranger."

He muttered, "Aw, mush!" and went on upstairs to fetch Clara's saddlebags. He didn't ask the Indian gal why she was crying like that when he passed by her again on his way out.

By the time he rejoined the white gals at the livery, a couple of other Leadville riders had come by to join forces with them. So he figured Clara and his messages to the outside world would make it safely over the pass. It wouldn't have been seemly to kiss the auburn-haired beauty in public, so they shook hands instead and he helped her up on her sidesaddle, once he'd lashed her baggage behind it.

He stood there in the morning sunlight, smoking a fresh cheroot as he stared wistfully after the great hips bouncing gracefully out of sight.

Then that posse led by the town deputy called Wes came in from the other direction, dog dirty and all ridden out after a futile search for sign. So once they'd unsaddled and seen to the creature comforts of their lathered mounts, Longarm joined them in the Lucky Seven for some of that beer they'd been jawing about on the trail for hours.

Wes said he wasn't all that surprised by the badge Longarm now wore openly, seeing Longarm had been pals with poor old Blackfoot and having seen him handle Hyena Harris. But the younger lawman was thunderstruck as Longarm brought him up to date on more recent events in Holy Cross.

Wes said he'd never even considered Big Jim Fagan, even after that Penn kid had shot Blackfoot Blake from the roof of Big Jim's hardware.

Longarm said, "I doubt there was any connection betwixt them. Penn was a Colorado rider. So it's possible he recognized me as I was on my way to jaw with your boss, and shinnied his way up to the nearest handy ambush. It's just as likely he was after your boss. Federal or local lawmen take

146

the same interests in a road agent."

Longarm thoughtfully sipped some suds before he added, "I hope you understand I have the power to deputize you, Ray, or any other honest cuss to serve under me as I hold the fort till we can get this township more organized, Wes?"

The younger lawman grinned. "Hell, I'd be proud to tell my grandchildren I rode under Longarm. But who are we riding after, Boss?"

Longarm said, "Ain't sure. Can't even say for certain that Big Jim Fagan was really One-Eyed Jack until I get some answers to some wires I asked a pal to send for me in Leadville. Meanwhile, this tiny town seems to be crawling with suspicious characters from far and wide. So I want to gather a few good men together and be ready for whatever in hell might be fixing to happen next!"

Chapter 15

What happened next was a meeting with the handful of bigger froggies that ran the small puddle on the less-settled side of the Divide. It was held in a back room at the Prospector's Trust where Longarm had been meaning to go over some bank records in any case.

Almost as soon as the meeting began, there was some concern about a federal lawman policing their mining boom. A toad-faced cuss in a herringbone suit said he was with Amalgamated Minerals, and that he wasn't at all happy about the way Longarm had already bullied one of his straw bosses.

Longarm said, "If we're talking about Hyena Harris, I wasn't out to bully him. He was out to bully me for no sensible reason, save for my being prettier, I reckon. If I thought he had the self-control, I'd deputize Hyena to help me get a handle on things here. But he don't. So I won't."

The Amalgamated man snapped, "Nobody's asking you to take our own hired help off the job, Deputy Long. You don't seem to get my point at all! The question before the house is what gives you the right to ride in from outside and just take over here!"

Longarm smiled thinly and replied, "This ain't no state legislature. It's an ad hoc committee of self-appointed gents in an unincorporated township, operating on public land under the federal regulations of the Mining Acts you mining magnates lobbied so hard for."

He let that sink in before he added firmly, "Meaning this ain't the California God Rush of '49, or even Pikes Peak in '58, meaning you ain't no vigilance committee and we're going to have some proper law and order around here. That'll be federal, meaning me, until I hear different from the federal government. I doubt I will until such time as you incorporate a constitutional local government and get chartered as a township by the state of Colorado with the blessings of Uncle Sam."

He tried not to be disrespectful as he growled in a softer tone, "It's the least you can do after helping yourself to all these former Indian holdings under the mighty generous terms of both state and federal mining regulations."

Cooper, the more pleasant banker Longarm had talked to the night before, said soothingly that everyone there was for law and order. So Longarm said, "*Bueno*. I want you to go over the books and give me a list of any checks bigger than a hundred dollars signed by the late James Fagan or Widow Lawford in, say, the last six months. Later this afternoon will be good enough."

The banker protested their Holy Cross branch hadn't been open six months. Longarm smiled and said, "That's even better. I'm most interested in property or mining claims they might have bought into."

A white-haired gent in a dusty black suit said, "I can tell you the answer to that question, Deputy Long. As justice of the peace and the one and only notary public for miles, licensed by the state of Colorado, by damn, I'd be the one to notarize such deals. So I can say without looking it up that Jim Fagan bought his building lot off Amalgamated Minerals, and contracted with Lem Winslow here to build his hotel and hardware. If he or his secret pal, that widow, bought into any other business around here, it was under the table, not on paper."

The construction contractor called Winslow nodded innocently. The frog in the herringbone suit looked more like a sheep now as Longarm smiled at him knowingly and said, "*Bueno*. The federal minerals act allows one to claim most any amount of surface land to get at most anything mineral that may lie under it. So who's to say it's a sin to sell off some of your surface claim after you've explored it. Haven't you started to fatten beef stock down the creek as well?"

The frog croaked, "I assure you we've done nothing we're not allowed to under current laws!"

Longarm nodded and dryly observed, "Doubt old boys like you will ever allow Washington to change 'em. There's this big real-estate tract near Denver, built on a mineral claim supposedly to mine pottery clay. It's been said the clay-mining syndicate ran off some fools who'd only filed homestead claims. Then what do you know, the clay mining proved unprofitable, so they put up tracts of frame cottages for sale instead. But like you just said, it was perfectly legal. So let's stick with what's raw enough in Holy Cross to inspire blood and slaughter."

He saw he had their undivided attention. "You gents here seem to have a lock on the water, timber, minerals, or plain open range for a good three miles or more in any direction. If I take you all at your words about the late Jim Fagan and Widow Lawford, what can any of you tell me about all the hardcase strangers that seem to be drifting in by the hour?"

When everyone looked blank, he snorted and said, "I am speaking, of course, of hired guns. This ain't the first boom town I've ever been through. I know for a fact the mining over this way has been fair to middling. I know nobody has full shifts working the try-holes still being worked. I know you don't mine shit with a six-gun, and the sort of gents we're talking about ain't good with any other sorts of tools.

So who's fixing to fight whom over what?"

Everyone there, and there were over a dozen, assured Longarm he knew nothing about mineral, water, or range disputes on that side of the Divide. More than one agreed he'd noticed the hardcase strangers Longarm had mentioned. Banker Cooper said, "We've hired our own extra guns out front. All army vets, if you'd care to ask them for credentials. But I don't think we're being cased for a robbery. I've been robbed, more than once. So you get to where you can tell."

Longarm allowed he'd noticed that, and agreed it was all mighty confounding. He asked a few more leading questions, but none of them led anywhere. So they agreed to talk about it later, and the meeting broke up pleasantly enough.

When Longarm saw dozens of pony rumps down the one main street in front of the town lockup, he naturally hurried down that way.

More men than ponies were gathered out front, some talking ugly about tar, feathers, and ropes. Longarm elbowed his way inside to find Wes and that other deputy, Ray, trying to calm down two score or more others crowded into the small office with them. Longarm glanced at the worried-looking prisoners behind the bars in the back, and drew his .44-40 to fire a round into the floorboards for attention.

As he got some, standing there in a cloud of dust and gunsmoke, he snapped, "Everyone but Wes and Ray outside or he goes back in the cells on the double. I don't give a shit either way."

They decided they'd as soon wait outside, although more than one grumbled, and one of them muttered, "Shit, there's three of them and all of us. How many of us could they hope to stop?"

A wiser head muttered back, "Fifteen at the most. You aim to go first, Chuck?"

So as soon as he was alone with his two junior deputies and the dispirited half-dozen prisoners eyeing him through

151

the park-bench-green bars, Longarm quietly asked, "Who brought Fandango and his pals in and on what charge?"

Ray said smugly, "I did. Me and my posse cut 'em off this side of the pass, and figured they might have been in on it with the Penn kid from Coal Creek."

Longarm muttered to himself, and refrained from reaching for another smoke as he ambled back to the cells. It would have been rude to light up without offering, and his smokes cost more than he figured Fandango and his sullen crew were worth to him.

He said, "Morning, Fandango. Before you say it, I know you and your pals here never rode into town with that Penn kid. For I met all you noisy assholes out on the range, and it's agreed Penn and his own pals were here earlier."

The Fandango Kid grumbled, "That's what we've been trying to tell everybody, speaking of assholes. Seeing you ain't half as dumb, when do we get out of here, damnit?"

"You don't want to step out front without some friend to vouch for you, Fandango. There's a hell of a crowd and they're all het up about sinister strangers here in Holy Cross. So why don't you tell us something I can tell them, explaining your mysterious presence?"

The Fandango Kid protested, "Damnit, we hadn't hurt nobody, and we were trying to *leave* when that loco posse threw down on us and hauled our innocent asses back!"

Longarm considered, shrugged, and turned to the other lawmen. "Why don't we just send 'em out on their own, seeing they're so innocent? I doubt anyone will really tar and feather anyone, do you?"

Wes smiled boyishly. "Of course they won't. They'll just rope 'em, drag 'em, and shoot 'em once they get 'em out of town a ways."

Behind him, The Fandango Kid insisted, "You're talking pure murder! You got no call to hand us over to no mob!

What have we ever done to you or your'n?"

Longarm said, "Nothing, for or against me, albeit I know at least one of you would sure like to clean my plow, because I heard him say so the other night. We wouldn't be doing a thing, one way or the other, if we just turned you boys loose. You just said we had no right to hold you, and it's not as if we *owed* you shit!"

The ashen-faced hardcase said, "All right. If you must know, we come over this way to play cards with Sky Kirby. You were there. You saw me win big off him!"

The puzzled federal man stared soberly through the bars and said, "I sure did. How did you manage that, Fandango? No offense, but whether we can prove it or not, you're probably better known as a drygulcher for fun and profit than a cardsharp. I was standing behind you. You took that pot with a bluff many a schoolmarm might have called."

The murderous Fandango Kid insisted, "Sky Kirby didn't. So I won, and you saw him write me that handsome check. I got it right here in my money belt if you want to examine it close!"

Longarm shook his head. "It's good or it ain't. A gambling man who'd bounce a check off someone like you would have to be even dumber than a high roller who bought a brass-balled bluff. Now tell us why you rode all the way over the Divide just to play cards with even Sky Kirby, Fandango."

The caged killer replied stubbornly, "When you want to play for high stakes you go where the high rollers are. I'd ride way farther than I just rode for another twenty grand. They say Doc Holliday just left Colorado for that new silver strike down Arizona way, and you know he's never been in no game with the likes of Sky Kirby!"

Longarm said, "Few of us have. Are you saying you heard there'd be some high rolling here, and rode all this way just to get in on it, not knowing shit about poker, no offense?"

The Fandango Kid smiled smugly and replied, "Let me be the judge of how well I know the game, once I cash Sky's check in Denver!"

Longarm grimaced and turned back to the junior deputies. "Ray, most of 'em out there seemed to have ridden under you. So you'd be the best one to calm 'em down. We're letting this bunch go. We'd be wise to give 'em an armed escort out of town and hand 'em back their own guns once they were well clear."

Ray protested, "We're letting 'em go just like that? What about poor old Blackfoot Blake?"

Longarm said, "They didn't do it. Would your dead soul rest easier if somebody avenged your death by lynching the wrong ones? Mine wouldn't. The trouble with blaming the wrong ones, aside from it being sloppy law enforcement, is that the guilty ones are still out there."

He pointed over his shoulder with a thumb as he added, "Like I said, I met these lowlifes out on the trail. Penn paid for gunning Blackfoot with his own life. The pals seen around town with him might or might not have been in on the gunplay with him. I'd as soon know what, or who, inspired Penn to be so noisy. So why not narrow the field some by sending these hardcases on their way and mayhaps see how many we've got left?"

Ray said he'd go out and have a word with the boys. Longarm told the prisoners to just sit tight for, say, another half hour. The Fandango Kid said, "You're a straight shooter, Longarm. If anyone ever offers me money to drygulch you, I'll try to remember this!"

Longarm said just as easily, "If you ever shoot me in the back, I'll never speak to you again."

Later, after Ray and some of his boys had left with The Fandango Kid and his pals, Wes marveled, "Jesus H. Christ, Longarm, didn't you hear Fandango confess right out that he shot gents in the back for money?"

Longarm nodded soberly. "I did. Proving that a true confession in court could be a pisser, though. Even if his lawyer was too dumb to say he'd only been joshing, you have to have a particular corpus delicti to go with a particular confession. You can't just say you heard Billy the Kid brag on killing twenty-one men, not counting niggers or greasers, the lying little shit. You got to prove he's killed one in particular. Last I heard, the murder warrant on Darling Billy only indicts him for back-shooting Sheriff William Brady of Lincoln County. There nothing about all the wonders and cucumbers him and his admirers crow about."

Wes said he'd keep an eye out for delicate corpses, and Longarm resisted the temptation to lecture a green hand some more on common law. There were elected judges who didn't seem to know corpus delicti meant the body of the crime, not a dead body, while smart-ass killers had swung because they'd been misinformed that the law couldn't touch you if you got rid of a dead body but left other evidence you'd done away with somebody.

But whether Longarm felt like lecturing on common law or not, he was reminded what somebody else had said about the best way to learn something being to try and teach it to somebody else. He knew he had more dead bodies than any certain crime! There was only his fairly firm conviction that Big Jim Fagan had been One-Eyed Jack McBride, and that Widow Lawford had betrayed Sean O'Hanlon to him before she'd been murdered in turn by the ruthless rascal.

After that, try as he might, he couldn't make the killing of Blackfoot Blake fit, if it made any sinister sense at all. Neither that kid from Coal Creek nor the older lawman he'd killed were in any position to say whether they'd had earlier words or not.

Young Ray came back inside, looking less worried as he declared, "We let Fandango and his pals go. But a whole new show just came to town."

Longarm cocked a questioning brow. Ray said, "The Gatewood boys, all of 'em. They just rid into Holy Cross with the announced intention of enjoying some high rolling of their own with the famous Sky Kirby, if he knows what's good for him."

Wes said, "Jesus, them three Gatewood brothers have been accused of everything but the clap, and I wouldn't want my sister marrying any of 'em anyways. Where's everybody now? Do you reckon Sky and his own boys will stand up to 'em or run for it?"

Ray said, "Can't say. Neither can anyone else. I told you it was a whole new show in town!"

Chapter 16

Longarm stepped out on the walk, got rid of his smoke, and headed for the Lucky Seven Saloon to see if anyone was dealing that early in the day, and if so, who.

He naturally had to pass Lawford's Last Post on the far side. So he wasn't surprised when little Columbine Owlfeather came out to tear across the street at him in her calico frock and linen apron.

The Kimoho gal looked more grown up, maybe as old as seventeen, in the harsh sunlight. All the Uto-Aztec-speaking nations tended to have short arms and legs for their natural-sized heads and trunks. It made them look sort of like cute babies when they were young, or oversized fat dwarves when they got old. It would have been rude to warn a worried-looking Indian gal to watch her weight when she got older, so he just howdied her and asked if he could be of any service.

Columbine said, "I just heard some more bad men had come to town, Saltu Ka Saltu! They are brothers. Three of them. I heard some other Saltu talking about them in the lobby just now. They said that it is Ike Gatewood you have to watch. He says nothing and seems not to care as his shorter brother, Matt, starts to argue with people."

Longarm nodded soberly and said, "It ain't such an original ploy, and I'd already heard how the Gatewoods shot up Lyons and Jimtown."

She insisted, "They have killed men, many. People say they have robbed and murdered lonely travelers they met on mountain trails as well!"

Longarm replied, "They ain't wanted on federal charges, and the state can't seem to prove its case against them on the rare occasions they stand trail. It's tough to find twelve good men who'd convict on circumstance with that many kith and kin of the accused attending the trail. Reckon the only way they'll ever calm down will involve somebody catching them in the act and willing to swear they resisted arrest."

He saw she seemed about to fall in beside him, and gently added, "I'd be proud to buy you a root beer if they served young ladies at the saloon I'm headed for, Miss Columbine. But they don't. So why don't you just go on back to the hotel and stay out of this noonday sun, hear?"

She said she would, adding, "I have cleaned up your room and replaced your shot-up mattress and bedding. I locked up with my passkey when I was done. So you don't have to worry about your things."

He thanked her, and almost put his hand in his jeans before he decided tipping her might be overdoing it after lending her that ten bucks he'd likely never see again. So he just ticked his hat brim to her and went on his way. There wasn't much of a ways to walk in any town the size of Holy Cross. So it only took him a few minutes to reach the Lucky Seven Saloon. There were better than a dozen ponies tethered out front. But when he stepped through the batwings he saw the tap room was nearly empty. So he bought himself a scuttle of plain draft at the bar and mosied for the back room, holding the heroic drink in his left hand.

He'd had the Gatewood boys pointed out to him in Boulder one night. So he had the three of them located in the crowd right off as he eased around to the back wall and sort of slid along it without drawing much attention to himself. For everyone there seemed intent on the game in progress.

Sky Kirby was dealing. Matt Gatewood was seated at the table with the high roller and two locals, including the humorous-talking old driller, Trevor Crockett. The quietly sinister Jake and Ike Gatewood, who was supposed to be the most dangerous, were standing behind their more boisterous baby brother, who'd just raised, drawing a collective gasp of wonder from the earlier arrivals.

There was room amid Kirby's less obvious backers for Longarm to make out the hand Kirby held if one started out tall and craned his neck a mite while sipping suds from a scuttle. Longarm had ordered the largest-sized vessel they served beer in with such a move in mind, knowing he might want to repeat it more than once.

Sky Kirby was holding a full house, Longarm saw, meaning it was not so wise to be standing in the line of fire should the beetle-browed Matt Gatewood question the odds of the dealer winding up with such a hand by pure chance.

Kirby saw Gatewood and raised him five hundred. Crockett stayed, but all the others, save for Matt Gatewood, folded. By this time Longarm had eased to one side with his eyes on sleepy-eyed Ike Gatewood, and since it was awkward to play casually with a cross-draw rig, he'd just drawn his .44-40 with the free hand hiding in the crowd to hold it down his right leg as he nursed his big beer in his left hand.

Matt Gatewood said sullenly, "I think you're bluffing. I'll see you and raise you a thousand!"

Trevor Crockett said he only owned a silver claim, not the U.S. Mint, and folded. That left the mean-eyed Matt and the silkier Sky smiling coldy at one another across an alarming pile of chips, and Longarm knew the suspected road agent needed at least a flush to beat the high roller's full house!

A long time went by in total silence. Then Sky Kirby sighed and placed his cards face down on the table, saying, "You win. I'll write you a check for those chips, Mister Gatewood."

Matt Gatewood said, "You do that, Mister High Roller, and then I mean to buy everyone here a drink with my winnings off you!"

Sky Kirby got out his pen and checkbook to pay up like a pro as he wistfully asked whether that invitation included him.

When Matt Gatewood said it did, in a gloating tone, some of the boys started heading out the door before Kirby could hand the ruffian's check across the table. Longarm just went on nursing his beer against the wall. It was Trevor Crockett who noticed the six-gun down at his side and sidled over, murmuring, "Trouble, Marshal?"

Longarm said, "Reckon not this time. You seem a good loser as well. What was that just now about you owning a silver mine? I was told you worked in the Blue Devil, no offense."

The Cousin Jack said, "None taken. I do work in the Blue Devil, and it's not a silver mine I bought from Kirby yet. It's only a try-hole he won off another good loser the other night. He offered to let me look it over first, of course. So I thought his asking price sounded fair. There's a little water at the bottom, and the chrysolite vein they were following is thinner than the soles of a tired boot, but it's high-grade ore and, what the hell, I've always wanted to be my own boss. So I'll be working my regular job and improving my very own claim by moonlight."

Longarm said it sounded tedious, and put away his gun before he followed the drift to the doorway, dryly observing, "It's none of my beeswax, old son, but was what you were doing just now the way you dig silver ore?"

160

Crockett said, "It is indeed. It takes money to work hardrock, even when you're drilling gold quartz! I spent almost all my savings buying that thin silver vein and a hell of a lot of bedrock from Sky Kirby. So I was trying to win some of it back, the more fool I."

"You mean you're tapped out total?" Longarm asked.

The driller smiled sheepishly. "Not quite. You saw me fold before I'd gone stone broke, and I still have my job at the Blue Devil to tide me over until I can get some backing for my Sly Fox. That's what I've decided to name my mine, after another back home in the tin country."

Longarm said it sounded as sensible as Last Chance or Lost Mule as he casually turned over one of the cards Matt Gatewood had placed face down on the table. It was the deuce of clubs. Longarm asked Trevor Crockett if they'd been playing deuces wild. The Cornishman shook his head and said, "Hell, poker gets wild enough when you leave the joker in the deck. Why do you ask?"

Longarm turned over another card and said, "He was holding a trash hand and bluffing with . . . Jesus, didn't Sky have to make good on every chip in that pot no matter who'd bet it?"

When the driller said of course, Longarm asked, "Then who got the money when you gents bought all them chips earlier?"

Trevor Crockett looked puzzled and said, "I don't know about the others. I naturally paid Kirby himself with a check. A man would be a fool to carry more than a few dollars in cash around a town as wild as this one."

Longarm scowled. "All right, you and others in town might be good for credit on paper. But nobody with the brains of a gnat would sell redeemable chips to a saddle tramp such as Gatewood!"

Crockett said he hadn't been watching, and suggested the strangers might have paid cash. Longarm shook his head.

"Would you accept all your winnings by check, drawn on a Denver bank, if you'd just handed Sky Kirby more than a thousand in cash right here in Holy Cross?"

Trevor Crockett whistled softly and said, "I don't believe I'd want to. But I might be afraid to insist. Just what are you getting at, Marshal?"

Longarm shrugged. "That's *Deputy* Marshal, and I wish I knew. I can't put my finger on anything illegal, but that still ain't no way to run a railroad! It makes no sense to gamble the way Sky Kirby's been gambling."

Crockett mildly observed that nobody had caught the high roller with his fingers in any cookie jars. Longarm said, "That's what I mean. It's a pure fact of nature that no professional gambler has ever made a living by giving suckers an even break or, in this case, a better-than-even break!"

By now they were out in the tap room, and Longarm had finished as much as his scuttle as he needed. So he reached between one of Sky Kirby's bunch and Ike Gatewood to put the big glass vessel on the bar. Ike Gatewood smiled sleepily at him and said, "Howdy, ah . . . Deputy. Noticed you in the back room with your gun out. Sort of hurt my feelings. Was you expecting trouble?"

Longarm met his gaze as warmly, softly saying, "I was. But Sky Kirby never saw fit to call your baby brother's bluff. So now I'd like the three of you to take your winnings and be out of town by sundown, Mister Gatewood."

The nearby Kirby man sucked in some breath, and crowded his pal on the far side to move farther down the bar as Ike Gatewood went on smiling and gently asked, "What if we call your bluff? You have no authority to run innocent gents out of town. What's the charge you might use as your excuse, even if you win?"

Longarm said, "Vagrancy. I'm acting pro tem under state as well as federal law till they can get a regular peace officer here. I'm sure you Colorado riders know that your own

162

Centennial State frowns on vagrancy and defines a vagrant as any drifter with no place of residence or visible means of support?"

Ike Gatewood said, "Shit, we're rooming with pals here in Holy Cross, and you just saw my baby brother win better than eight grand back there!"

It didn't work on Longarm. He said, "Give me the names of any Holy Cross resident ready to vouch for you boys as guests or hired help, then show me some money, not no check, or get out of town by sundown unless you'd like to spend the night locked up as common vagrants."

He turned away without waiting to hear what the known troublemaker meant to make out of that. He knew he'd just bent the Bill of Rights a bit in the interest of peace and quiet. So seeing he had some other legal questions as well, he went next to the nearby office of that J.P. and notary, where "Justice Jethro Marcy" appeared in new gilt letters on the second-story door above the row of shops below.

The same old white-haired gent he'd spoken to at the bank was at a rolltop desk, alone in his small office, as Longarm strode in. The J.P. indicated one of the two other chairs in the place, and asked Longarm what he needed notarized.

Longarm sat down, saying, "Nothing yet. I was hoping you might be able to clear up some questions for me, though."

Old Marcy leaned back expansively and said to shoot. So Longarm told him what he'd just said to Ike Gatewood.

The J.P. chuckled and said, "That's the way to handle such pests. Blackfoot Blake would have bought 'em drinks and told them tales of taming wilder towns and whole tribes of Indians. If they refuse to ride out, you'd do better just shooting 'em than trying to make your charge stick, though. They do hail from some home spread somewhere in Colorado. On the other hand, how were you supposed to know that when you tried to run them in and they resisted arrest? Get plenty of backing and make sure you drop Ike first, though."

It might have sounded like bragging to say he preferred to work alone at such odds. So Longarm said, "As long as I'm here, I just talked to Trevor Crockett and he tells me Sky Kirby just sold him a silver claim. They'd want to record such a sale with you, wouldn't they?"

Marcy nodded. "They might not want to, but they sure would have to ask me to notarize the sale. I got my own copy right in that file cabinet behind you. Kirby won the claim off Lem Boggs a few nights ago. Old Lem's a good prospector but a foolish card player. Kirby knows he's no mining man. So he sold the claim to a man who is, for ten thousand. I recall all this because I only recorded the sale a couple of days ago."

Longarm said he'd take the older man's word for what he had in his own files and declared, "Old Sky sure wheels and deals in silver claims. He tried to tell us he sold another hole in the ground for ten times more. You naturally wouldn't have witnessed his famous sale to Miss Clara Drakmanton, right?"

The J.P. looked confused and answered, "Sure I would. It ain't every day I notarize a hundred-thousand-dollar sale."

A large gray cat got up and turned around in Longarm's gut as he softly said, "You mean, she *bought* his hole in the ground, just as he'd bet her she would, for a hundred thousand dollars?"

Marcy said uncertainly, "Never heard about no bet. They just came here together yesterday, by gum, and had me notarize the transfer of property for 'em. I got a copy, if you'd care to see it."

Longarm said he sure would, and rose to make room for the older man. Marcy opened a middle drawer, rummaged a time, and announced, "That's funny. Funny as hell. I had her right here, filed under the letter D for Drakmanton and . . . damn it to hell, some damned body has been in this damned office overnight!"

He sprang over to his desk, unlocked a side drawer with a key from his pocket, and heaved a sigh of relief as he said, "Now it gets even crazier! Nothings been taken from my cash drawer, yet they lifted half a dozen folders from my files over there! What in thunder would anyone want with property transfers and such?"

Longarm said, "It beats me, sir. Copies or even originals would do a thief little good against titleholders with witnesses in any court of law. What if they just wanted to know who owned what and . . . Never mind. They'd only have to ask to see the county register. So like I've been saying all along, none of this makes a lick of common sense on the surface."

He put a hand on the doorknob and added, "I reckon I'd best go turn over some more rocks."

The J.P. followed him to the door, asking where he was headed next. Longarm said he didn't know. "Where do you head when you're totally lost in a swamp? Just around in circles asking more dumb questions, I reckon. If I had any notion what I've been missing here in Holy Cross I might ask smarter ones!"

Down on the street again, he stopped at a tamale stand and washed down two tamales with some stale black coffee. It failed to make him think any better. But he stuck to coffee and tobacco, and he avoided liquor for the rest of the day as he almost literally ran in circles, asking folks he'd talked to before and some he'd never met before about most everything he could come up with in the hopes of forming some sensible pattern.

He was having supper at that sit-down across from the hotel when his junior deputy, Wes, caught up with him. Wes sat down with Longarm, and allowed he'd have some chili too. Then as they were eating, Wes softly said, "Heard we were fixing to run the Gatewood boys out of town as well. What if they don't want to go?"

Longarm said, "Let me worry about it. That's an order and I mean it. You've surely heard about the time a deputy of James Butler Hickok ran up behind him unexpectedly during a personal fight in uncertain surroundings. I don't want you or Ray anywhere near if and when I have to nudge those unwelcome strangers on their way."

The younger lawman said quietly, "There'd be three of them and one of you, right?"

Longarm replied as quietly, "There's fifteen rounds in the magazine, and I can get one in the chamber of my Winchester before I go roaming in the gloaming. Nobody does that with no more than his six-gun when he's expecting trouble."

Wes said, "They'll be expecting you. They don't know me and Ray. What if we was to work our way close with shotguns and . . ."

"That would be premeditated murder and I'd have to charge you with it," Longarm told him. "I got to give 'em a chance to go quiet or come quiet if they'd rather spend some time in jail. It ain't that I'm a good sport. I'm a professional lawman and there are rules we're all supposed to . . . You know, that's the smartest thing I've said for some time!"

Wes asked what he meant. Longarm said, "Sky Kirby ain't been playing by professional rules, or even the rules of a tyro out to take home half his marbles. He's been playing slick as hell about mining claims whilst letting owlhoot riders take him like a chump for heavy cash. Or has he been? I can see how a man could get famous fast as a good loser. But-A-Million-Gates advertises all the times he's lost and paid off handsome. But he don't make a habit of it, and you seldom hear about the rich old boys he beats. Most sporting gents don't like to talk about their losses. It's the professionals who want it known they pay off a sucker now and again."

Wes nodded sagely and said, "Like once in a blue moon."

It had been a statement rather than a question. But Longarm had to nod and say, "More like once or more a day when you're

166

playing against Sky Kirby. It's almost as if he's attracting them other high rollers the way an open honey pot draws flies. I don't care how often a man might wheel and deal in mining claims or silver futures. There ain't no way you can gamble away thirty grand or more in less than forty-eight hours and still stay solvent!"

Wes started to tell the tale of Leadville Brown's famous horse race with Silver Dollar Tabor, but Longarm said he'd heard it and added, "Like you said, once in a blue moon. Nobody can make a regular habit of losing big money and not go broke."

He left a tip on the table and went across to the hotel to get his Winchester as the shadows commenced to lengthen along the one main street.

Chapter 17

When he unlocked his room upstairs, he saw Columbine had put an extra quilt at the foot of the bed and left a mason jar filled with yellow daisy-like flowers on the bed table. He smiled as he sat on the bed to check the action and load of his well-oiled Winchester '73. He could see why some old mountain men such as the Bents and Kit Carson had never married up with white gals after spending a time as squaw men. It wasn't that all Indian gals were nicer than all white gals. But you generally knew when an Indian gal was sore enough at you to stab you in the back. It hurt to think he'd been wrong about that violet-haired widow and pretty Clara Drakmanton both.

He lit a cheroot and just sat there, staring out the window as he gave the setting sun and the Gatewood boys all the time they might need while he muttered aloud, "If you had a lick of sense you wouldn't worry about all this other mysterious shit. Old Billy Vail sent you over here to see if you could find One-Eyed Jack, not to save the world. You've got as solid a case for that Big Jim Fagan being One-Eyed Jack McBride, as well as the killer of our informant and his sneaky female partner, as you'll ever be able to build on this side of the Divide. For what will you bet on your chances of ever hearing from that lying Clara Drakmanton again?"

He rose to his feet, straightened his hat, adjusted his .44-40 to ride better on his hip, and stepped out in the hall with his Winchester. He locked up and went downstairs, meaning to thank little Columbine for the flowers. But she wasn't there. So he stepped outside in the sunset, took a deep breath of the thin mountain air, and started looking for the Gatewood boys.

He failed to find them. He checked all the saloons along the street, and nobody had seen them that evening. When he asked at the Lucky Seven, they told him Sky Kirby hadn't come back from his supper at the private home he'd paid to board at. Nobody seemed to know where that was either. But they said they expected him back before nine, to play serious cards with some gent called Bart the Boots. Longarm said he'd be back. He'd heard of Bart the Boots. Nobody could prove he'd really stomped that whore to death over in Durango, but it promised to be an interesting game and it was already after eight.

The first stars were winking when Wes met up with him near the livery and said, "I just asked. They mounted up before sundown and rode, like you told 'em to. The livery hands say that high roller, Sky Kirby, picked up his own mount to ride off somewhere just a few minutes ago. He didn't say where, but he took some of his boys with him."

Longarm frowned thoughtfully and said, "There's yet another hardcase cuss expecting to play cards with him within the hour. Maybe that was what he wanted to avoid. I'd best go ask Bart the Boots when he shows up for the game."

Wes marveled, "That mad-dog killer from Durango's here in Holy Cross tonight? Jesus H. Christ, what do they do, send out engraved invitations to this out-of-the-way neck of the woods?"

Longarm smiled thinly, told Wes he could be right, and headed back the way he'd just come. As he passed his hotel he considered whether he still wanted to pack his saddle gun along. He decided he might as well. They hadn't said Bart the Boots was alone, and even by himself he was said to have killed fourteen people, some of them grown men. It was women and unarmed men he used his famous boot heels on. He was said to treat armed men with the respect they deserved.

But back at the Lucky Seven Saloon, things seemed quiet as any weeknight on the hungry side of payday. Those drinking at the bar, including that old J.P. Marcy, tended to be better-dressed gents who could afford to drink any night in the week. When Longarm asked the barkeep, he was told nothing was going on in the back yet. The barkeep agreed they'd been looking forward to a spell of high rolling. But here it was almost eight, and neither Sky Kirby nor Bart the Boots had shown up yet.

Since the old J.P. seemed curious, Longarm explained the odd lack of action to him. When Marcy said he found it less interesting than the theft of those papers from his office, Longarm told him, "All the folks you served have their own copies. I know it'll be a bother. But you can doubtless wind up with new certified copies after a time if you take the time to approach 'em about it as they come by with other stuff they want notarized."

The older man brightened and declared, "You're right. Smart too. I'd already thought of that, but most folks don't know exactly how a notary public works."

Longarm signaled the barkeep for a round, and said any federal lawman had to know a tad more about such matters than most, being called upon to testify in all sorts of courts across the land.

The older man still seemed unhappy about all the fuss, and kept badgering Longarm for answers he just didn't have as it slowly got to be eight and then later.

There was no sign of Sky Kirby or his bodyguards. If they'd run from one man, they must have thought he was one tough son of a bitch. Longarm reviewed the little he really knew about the shady Bart the Boots. A killer anyone knew a lot about was generally in jail, if he hadn't been sentenced to the rope dance. So all that was known for certain about Bart the Boots was his odd handle. There were rumors that his terrible temper was under better control than he let on. As a pimp-extortionist, a bullyboy saved a lot of needless sweat by keeping others on edge and in terror of an unpredictable rage. There was nobody raging in the place at the moment. A couple of local boys seemed unhappy about the lack of entertainment that evening. But as many more just leaned against the bar or sat at tables, quietly drinking another lonesome evening away.

Longarm felt the call to nature and excused himself to go take a leak.

It was silly, he knew, but he still had the muzzle of his saddle gun proceeding him as he came back across the yard. It was still close. For he naturally took the other cuss coming out the back door for another man heeding the call to nature, till he saw the stranger in trail duds already had drawn and started to aim a double-action S&W as he pleasantly said, "Evening. Is this the way to the pisser?"

Longarm didn't answer. He let his Winchester do his talking for him as he fired with its muzzle only inches from the shirtfront of the total stranger!

The sweet-talking slicker still managed to blow a crater of cinders and gravel from the yard right next to Longarm's left boot as he flew backwards as far as the back-door steps and sprawled there like a stringless puppet with its shirt on fire.

His gray Stetson had fluttered to the cinders closer by. So Longarm bent to scoop it up as he yelled, "Don't nobody come through that damn door before I figure out who the hell is on my side!"

Then he moved on to beat out the flames on a dying man's chest with the dying man's hat, muttering, "Bart the Boots, I presume?"

The stranger he'd just shot never opened his eyes as he muttered back, "Jesus, they warned me you were good, but that was impossible! How did you do that when I was all primed up and had the drop on you?"

Longarm said, "It's a gift, I reckon. Who pointed me out in there and sent you after me? One hand washes the other, and I can see you get a swell coffin with a real stone marker, pard."

Bart the Boots never answered. Longarm felt the side of his neck and muttered, "Shit. I would have aimed higher and never let you get off the one shot if I'd known you were going to act like a dying clam on me!"

He rose back to his feet, levered another round in the chamber, and eased inside to find the tap room just about empty. This failed to astound him. Everybody wanted to gape at the *results* of a gunfight, but nobody wanted to be hauled into court as an unpaid witness.

He told the barkeep, "I'll take your word you never knew that cowhand in the front corner was a hired gun if you'll keep an eye on him whilst I round up some of my own pals!"

The barkeep didn't argue. Longarm moved out to the walk to see that, sure enough, windows and doors were popping open all up and down the street. He stepped off the walk to stand in a pool of lamplight, expecting both his junior deputies to come running to the not-too-distant echoes of gunplay and not wanting either to mistake him for anyone else with a Winchester held at port arms.

So his back made a swell target, as he realized with a chill of mortified chagrin when a gunshot rang out behind him too close for comfort!

Longarm crabbed for the shadows of the boardwalk as he was still whirling and swinging his saddle gun to fire from the hip at a far smaller blur about thirty yards off in the gloom. Then he noticed someone closer, sprawled face down in the dust and writhing like a wiggle worm caught out on a flagstone walk by sunrise. As he read the intent of that Colt Dragoon Conversion in the dust close to the sprawled figure, little Columbine Owlfeather came running toward him with her own smoking pepperbox in hand, sobbing, "I had to shoot him! He was about to shoot you in the back, Saltu Ka Saltu!"

They met above her writhing victim. Longarm handed the Indian gal his Winchester and drew his .44-40 as he hunkered down to roll the back-shot bastard over, whistle softly, and say, "Evening, Justice Marcy. I *know* good help is hard to find, but don't you think this was sort of dumb for a slick old bird like you?"

The old J.P. was bleeding from the mouth as he glared up at them with mingled bitterness and pain and gurgled, "*Somebody* had to do you, and nobody but Bart the Boots had the nerve to try. We had it made till you showed up to stick your damned federal nose in a purely local charade!"

Longarm said not unkindly, "Had not it been me, somebody else as smart as even Blackfoot Blake would have asked the same questions. Were those other kids riding with that Penn kid from Coal Creek in on Blake's killing, old son?"

Marcy only managed to blow some bubbles up as they were joined by Wes, Ray, and a couple of those gents Longarm had met earlier at the bank. Wes gasped, "Lord have mercy, who shot Marcy?"

The Indian gal sobbed, "I had to. I heard there were bad men in town, and when Saltu Ka Saltu wouldn't let me come with him, I got my father's old gun and followed!"

Wes asked, "Longarm, do you know what she's talking about?"

173

Longarm gently closed Marcy's glazed eyes with his fingers as he nodded and said, "Yep. There's another one ahint the saloon I got to shoot personal. From what Marcy just confessed, I'd say he had nobody left after that and found my back too tempting."

Longarm smiled up at the flustered Indian gal and added, "He'd have done me to death and likely got away with it if it hadn't been for my brave Kimoho partner here."

For some reason she started to cry. Longarm rose and took back his Winchester as he told his junior deputies, "Gutless wonders are no emergency. I'll put some wires out on Sky, the Gatewoods, and Fandango when I get back to a town with a Western Union. In the meanwhile I'd like a word with Trevor Crockett, if you boys know where he might be found."

A. M. Cooper of Prospector's Trust called out from back in the growing crowd. "I got him right here, Longarm. Don't you think of running, Cousin Jack. For this here derringer can reach way farther than a jackrabbit could get before I fired!"

Longarm yelled, "Don't shoot him. We want a statement from at least one of 'em to tie up all the loose ends!"

As the banker and another burly businessman marched the sheepishly grinning driller over to Longarm, Wes marveled, "Loose ends? I'll be whipped with snakes if I can make a lick of sense out all this noisy flimflam!"

Longarm said, "Neither could I, until Miss Columbine hit the deer in the eye just now!"

Young Ray, hunkered down by the dead man, frowned up at them. "No offense, Longarm, but this don't look like no deer and she got him betwixt the spine and left shoulder blade, not his eye."

Longarm shrugged and said, "I was speaking symbolic. Have any of you ever been hunting in tanglewood, staring ahead at nothing much, until you suddenly spot a shiny deer's

174

eye staring back at you from midair?"

Wes was the one who gasped. "I have and I follow your drift! One minute there's nothing there. Then you spot an eye, an antler tine, or whatever, and the whole damned deer falls into shape before your eyes, where it's been standing all the time!"

Longarm said that was what he'd meant, turned to Trevor Crockett, and said, "I want you to listen tight before you feed me any more fibs, Cousin Jack. I can prove you lied to me before, if I want to sit through your trial. But the charge would only be obstructing justice, and I'd be willing to save more time for you than me if you'd quit obstructing justice."

The Cornishman stared down at their dead ringleader as he said, "I don't know what you're talking about. I don't know what Justice Marcy was up to that might have been against the law. I don't see any proof that I was in on anything with him!"

Longarm sighed. "There you go obstructing justice some more. Of course there's nothing in the files at his office saying a man making no more than three dollars a day, no offense, and hanging out in saloons every night, had thousands of dollars saved up to buy a worthless mining claim."

"My Sly Fox is not worthless, look you!" the co-conspirator protested. "The high grade is there. It only needs a bit of . . ."

"Toad squat!" Longarm snapped. "Sorry, Miss Columbine. But I do forget my manners when they lie like that when I am trying to give them a break."

Then he said, "I got you cold, you poor simp. No jury of mortal mining men would ever believe an experienced mining man would buy an abandoned claim off a tinhorn who claimed he'd won it, and then show up in court without a shred of documentation!"

Crockett whimpered, "I have the bill of sale at my boarding-house! Signed by Sky Kirby, witnessed by Morgan Jenkins, and notarized by that poor old cuss you just shot for some reason!"

Longarm said, "He got shot for a good reason, and I was hoping to come up with some evidence as solid as you can provide. Marcy made up a story about lots of papers he didn't want me to see. I reckon you didn't know Morgan Jenkins is another shady rider a heap of lawmen would like to talk to about certain other transactions. I don't know, yet, whether Marcy really destroyed a heap of evidence or just hid it until he could have me killed, like Blake. In either case, as I was saying, we're going to lock you up for the night before we search your quarters for that fake property transfer, and I strongly advise you to see the light and make a full statement by sunrise. For do you go on lying to me in front of witnesses like this, I can likely add a charge of criminal conspiracy to obstructing justice."

Then he turned back to the ones on his side to get things in Holy Cross tidied up. It didn't take Trevor Crockett a whole night in jail to come clean and make a full statement, in writing.

Chapter 18

Less than a week later a homely but fancy-dressed butler let Longarm into the Drakmanton mansion in Pueblo, and showed him to the study, where the auburn-haired Clara had been reading with her hair down for the night.

Once they were alone in one another's arms Clara gasped, "Oh, Custis, I've been so worried about you! I had answers to all those wires you wanted me to send days ago. I paid a rider to carry them over the pass to you and . . ."

"We met above timberline," Longarm said, kissing her before he continued. "Gave me some interesting reading on the trail. I sent out some other wires as soon as I got into Leadville this afternoon."

She leaned the other way, purring, "Not on the sofa, silly. I have a full bedroom suite just up the stairs, and what do you mean by darkening my door at this late hour if you got in this afternoon?"

He said, "I just told you. Had to send some wires out on wanted outlaws scattered from here to breakfast. None of them were willing to go up against this child when push came to shove. But I do feel we ought to round up the likes of Sky Kirby, the Gatewoods, and a dozen other owlhoot riders before they really hurt somebody."

She put a finger to his lips and led him back over to the study door, saying, "Later. I want to hear all about it after you screw me silly!"

So they slipped out into the deserted hall and up the carpeted steps to the bedroom where he screwed her for the next hour in a variety of positions, one of which was new to her. But then, since all things good or bad must end, she wanted to hear all about the confusion in Holy Cross while they got their second winds.

As they lay naked together, propped up on lilac-scented pillows and sharing a three-for-a-nickel smoke, Longarm told her, "In the beginning there was One-Eyed Jack McBride, and that part wasn't all that confusing. McBride gunned another poker player and ran off with a solid fortune in Indian Agency funds. Somewhere along the line he fell in with Lavinia Miller, an outlaw's widow who ran a boardinghouse in Julesberg for riders on the dodge. Neither one was getting any younger, so they decided to start over in a remote mining town with the proceeds of their earlier sins. He became the respectable Big Jim Fagan whilst she turned into an army widow named Lawford."

Clara snuggled closer and asked, "Why did he slit her throat so wickedly then?"

Longarm said, "You're getting ahead of the story. First a barkeep named Sean O'Hanlon recognized McBride from somewhere in the past, but failed to see his kindly landlady was in cahoots with the hardware dealer next door. So he confided in her, she told McBride, and that was the end of O'Hanlon. Nobody might have ever figured that one out if they hadn't had that falling out that resulted in both of them winding up dead."

Clara asked, "Why do you suppose they quarreled, and what made him go after you once he'd murdered her? You had no idea who he was, and surely he had no other motive for killing you, did he?"

Longarm took a deep drag and weighed his words before he said, "He might have just got proddy when he saw *me*, of all unwelcome visitors, checking in with his secret partner. It must have spooked him to have the town law gunned from his very rooftop to begin with, and then one thing led to another till his guilty conscience drove him over a cliff. At any rate, that was that, and I'd have headed back sooner if it hadn't been for those other rascals drawing my attention to them with their own clever stunts."

Clara took a drag on their shared cheroot before she demanded he clear that part up, saying, "I really did pick up my winnings when I got back to Leadville, darling. How could Sky Kirby hope to come out ahead by throwing money around so thoughtlessly?"

Longarm explained, "A heap of thought went into it. Sky Kirby, like you and a driller called Crockett, was just a tool of the old slicker who set it up, a justice of the peace called Marcy."

She kissed his bare chest casually and allowed she'd never heard of Justice Marcy. To which he replied, "I know. He just said you had. They had to account for all the money Sky Kirby seemed to be losing at honest high rolling to other sporting gents. So they faked up a drawer full of bills of sale, showing Sky Kirby was wheeling and dealing in silver when he wasn't betting thousands and paying off his losses with worthless checks."

She brightened and said, "That's right. One of those answers to your earlier wires said the Kirby checking account in Denver would never cover more than a thousand dollars."

He took a drag of his own on their cheroot and explained, "That didn't matter. None of them big winners meant to cash any checks. They already had the cash, less a handsome commission for Justice Marcy, of course. It was all flimflam, designed to account for any sinister young man

179

with no visible means of support having a heap of spending money just the same."

She seemed confused. So he told her, "Most outlaws blow all the money they steal on cheap booze and expensive women, knowing they can't hardly invest it in stocks, bonds, or property lest somebody ask where it came from. So a wily old coyote who'd wandered all over the high country with a notary seal in his hand put together a sly proposition for the shadowy souls he knew from all over."

Clara oohed and said, "Of course! I know what you mean about the questions people ask when you bid big money on property. Gambling for big money is perfectly legal in Colorado, and as long as one could produce witnesses willing to swear they'd seen you win a whole lot of . . . your own ill-gotten gains?"

Longarm said, "That's about the size of it. Marcy charged a commission to set up a well-witnessed game with a known professional gambler. Lest anyone question how Sky Kirby could lose more money than he won, a licensed notary was in fine shape to whip up proof the high roller had won valuable claims and sold them for handsome profits. Marcy was about the only one over in Holy Cross with complete records on real wheeling and dealing. Everybody had him notarize their wheeling and dealing, but they never had call to compare notes. So he simply let Sky win abandoned claims off losers who'd already left town, then sell them at a profit to others, fictitious for the most part, with just a few real folks to throw off anyone who nosed around. I don't know what poor old Blackfoot Blake stuck his nose into, but he'd have naturally voiced his first suspicions to the local justice of the peace, and we can see what that did for his health. The Penn gang was in town to convert the contents of a strongbox into poker winnings. But old Marcy had another proposition for 'em. So Penn wound up dead, and his scared pals won't get all that far."

Clara asked how she and that crazy bet fit in.

Longarm said, "That was Sky Kirby's own grand notion, and it must have made the old sly coyote he was working for mad as hell. He'd told Sky to see if he could recruit some other real folks to pretend to buy holes in the ground, the way they'd recruited Crockett. But Sky overdid it when he used some of the working money old Marcy'd supplied to entice a famous rich lady over the pass, hoping to be as famous after bragging about getting a hundred grand out of one of the few real folks he could name who might have that sort of money to bet on silver futures."

She sighed. "You mean he wasn't after my innocent derriere?"

Longarm chuckled and said, "Not many men would turn it down. But I got in his way, and after old Marcy told him to send you home fast and safe, to get you out of an already tricky game, Sky tried to use me to back his brag that you'd bought his coyote hole for all that money. They didn't know about our own understanding, and only had me down as a harmless saddle tramp called Ginger."

She removed the cheroot from his lips and got rid of it as she purred, "I see how their story ends. So let's see if we can't just get your ginger up again. Did you miss me as much as I missed you these past lonely nights, you horny thing?"

He told her he sure had. It would have only upset a good old gal to hear how he'd learned that new position she liked from good old Columbine Owlfeather.

Watch for

LONGARM AND THE BOUNTY HUNTERS

187th novel in the bold LONGARM series
from Jove

Coming in July!

If you enjoyed this book, subscribe now and get...

TWO FREE

A $7.00 VALUE—

If you would like to read more of the very best, most exciting, adventurous, action-packed Westerns being published today, you'll want to subscribe to True Value's Western Home Subscription Service.

Each month the editors of True Value will select the 6 very best Westerns from America's leading publishers for special readers like you. You'll be able to preview these new titles as soon as they are published, *FREE* for ten days with no obligation!

TWO FREE BOOKS

When you subscribe, we'll send you your first month's shipment of the newest and best 6 Westerns for you to preview. With your first shipment, two of these books will be yours as our introductory gift to you absolutely *FREE* (a $7.00 value), regardless of what you decide to do. If

you like them, as much as we think you will, keep all six books but pay for just 4 at the low subscriber rate of just $2.75 each. If you decide to return them, keep 2 of the titles as our gift. No obligation.

Special Subscriber Savings

When you become a True Value subscriber you'll save money several ways. First, all regular monthly selections will be billed at the low subscriber price of just $2.75 each. That's at least a savings of $4.50 each month below the publishers price. Second, there is never any shipping, handling or other hidden charges—*Free home delivery*. What's more there is no minimum number of books you must buy, you may return any selection for full credit and you can cancel your subscription at any time. A TRUE VALUE!

A special offer for people who enjoy reading the best Westerns published today.

WESTERNS!

NO OBLIGATION

Mail the coupon below

To start your subscription and receive 2 FREE WESTERNS, fill out the coupon below and mail it today. We'll send your first shipment which includes 2 FREE BOOKS as soon as we receive it.

Mail To: **True Value Home Subscription Services, Inc. P.O. Box 5235**
120 Brighton Road, Clifton, New Jersey 07015-5235

YES! I want to start reviewing the very best Westerns being published today. Send me my first shipment of 6 Westerns for me to preview FREE for 10 days. If I decide to keep them, I'll pay for just 4 of the books at the low subscriber price of $2.75 each; a total $11.00 (a $21.00 value). Then each month I'll receive the 6 newest and best Westerns to preview Free for 10 days. If I'm not satisfied I may return them within 10 days and owe nothing. Otherwise I'll be billed at the special low subscriber rate of $2.75 each; a total of $16.50 (at least a $21.00 value) and save $4.50 off the publishers price. There are never any shipping, handling or other hidden charges. I understand I am under no obligation to purchase any number of books and I can cancel my subscription at any time, no questions asked. In any case the 2 FREE books are mine to keep.

Name

Street Address   Apt. No.

City   State   Zip Code

Telephone

Signature
(if under 18 parent or guardian must sign)

Terms and prices subject to change. Orders subject
to acceptance by True Value Home Subscription
Services, Inc.   **11391-3**